CATH'S CHOICE
A HISTORICAL ROMANCE

JOHANA GARDENER

plicit Press
Erotica Fiction

CHAPTER 1

CATH'S CHOICE-THE BEGINNING

HE REMEMBERS it like it was yesterday. The festival of Beltaine was upon them, but Ailill was not in the mood for celebrations. He was about to bury his wife, the mother of his only child. It was a solemn time.

The Druids were busy for the most part, invoking the god of the herd and harvest, hoping to ensure abundant crops, and a prolific harvest. But Ailill's heart was heavy with grief, saddened by the loss of his beloved Edain.

Edain had died young, much too young, and seemingly without cause. She was the picture of health the day before. And then suddenly and without warning, she was dead. If she had been ill, or perhaps if she had died in childbirth, it would have been acceptable. But she had simply fallen over, after giving her young child to a nursemaid, and died, without explanation.

The festival marked the beginning of summer, and it would be a sad summer for Ailill. How would he explain to his only child, one day when she was old enough to under-stand, that her mother had just died. There were really more things in heaven and on earth than could ever be understood. And with the Druids not being able to offer up an explanation for her untimely death, it was a day that Ailill dreaded.

He chose the perfect spot to lay her to rest, near a hill where they had met. She looked like she was sleeping like she would at any moment wake up and wonder at the fuss. But this did not happen, and as he watched them line her grave with jewels, urns, and her favorite mirror, as he watched them lower his wife into the ground, so beautiful on her ceremonial cart, he could not hold back from weeping.

But that was a long time ago, and his daughter is now a young woman. Ailill never remarried, and never had more children. So Cath, his only daughter, is a source of joy and pride for the nobleman. They meet, as is their custom, for an afternoon ride. Cath is quite an accomplished rider.

"Father, what news?" She always greets him the same way, as though a million things might have happened in the time since last they rode the day before.

"Nothing my child, save for the preparations for Beltaine, which are underway, and near completion." Ailill always managed an enthusiastic response, something which had become quite normal with the passage of time.

The festival of Beltaine, once again upon them, has always brought back memories of Ailill's greatest loss, and it has not gotten any better with the passage of time. He hurts today like he did that day. But it is a festival for the people, one which he must be seen to partake in, for fear of inciting the wrath of the gods.

They ride around the settlement, observing all the goings-on. The Druids are hard at work again, making sure that everything will be ready on time. It really is a spectacle to behold, and Cath loves the ceremony of it all.

She was young when her mother died; too young. So she cannot remember her the way her father does. She just has stories to go on, about her beauty and her heart. How her handmaiden would comb through her hair, red-gold in color, while she observed herself in her polished bronze mirror. Cath is nothing like her mother in this respect; as beautiful, more even, but she has always been more comfortable on a horse, mock-fighting with the men in the settlement.

At dawn, the Druids complete the rites that will result in the prosperity and fruitfulness of the New Year. Bonfires of oak and green yew topped by maypoles, rage in close proximity. These symbolize the sacred oak tree. Cattle pass between them as a Druid offers up sacred cakes to the harvest god, entreating him to purify the beasts with the pungent smoke.

Beneath oak branches hung with torques and bracelets offered by the faithful, the chief Druid lifts his arms in prayer to the god. A younger seer kneels down and divines omens from a human skull. These solemn rites will be followed by a joyful feast, a fair, and a day of sports.

The night before was unsettling though. In the night dividing spring and summer, the Druids placated the god with gifts and incantations, afraid that their luck might turn, or their cattle become bewitched. Severed heads were deemed an appropriate sacrifice to Belenos. But now, at dawn, the cattle were driven through the smoke of the sacred fires, purifying them, assuring them health and fertility.

With the festivities now in full swing, Ailill and Cath ride through the settlement, confident of a good year now that all the rights have been performed. They watch the sports and the feasting. Everyone is happy, and so they too are happy. Ailill, with all the heaviness in his heart, manages a smile for most of the day.

"It's wonderful, isn't it father?" Cath always gets excited around festival time.

"Yes, truly magnificent!" He says this looking away into the distance when the sun has already begun its descent from the sky, uncertain if he wants to weep, and needing therefore to be separated from his daughter.

As the sun sets, they meet Eogan, and Cath's father sees his chance to escape to the quietness of his house where he can mourn in peace. Eogan is tall, heavy set. He has piercing gray eyes set perfectly on his rough face, framed by golden locks. Ailill greets him, talks with him briefly, and then rides in the direction of home, leaving the two to discuss their future.

They reach the river just as the sun sets, catching the glistening orb as it fades behind the horizon. In the dark, it suddenly takes them a moment to adjust their eyes. But when they do, they are staring deep into one another's eyes, love hanging between them like fruit on a tree. It's tangible.

"I haven't seen you all day," Cath lies. She has watched very closely as Eogan won every fight, every race during the sports that day.

"Is that so?" He pulls her to him, a sly smile on his face, letting her know that he doesn't believe her. They might not have spoken at all that day. But she definitely saw him, him watching her, fighting for her, dueling for her. Everything that he does has a special resonance now that he has made everything in his life about her.

He kisses the side of her face and breathes in the smell of her hair. She lets him, wishing that he would inhale her so that she became a part of him. She wants to be a part of him, his everything, and he wants the same.

They share these feelings without saying anything to one another. They just inhale each other, knowing that soon, very soon they will be one. And it is the promise of this oneness that keeps them both looking forward to the future.

After a long time, Eogan creates just enough distance between them so that she can speak. Him too. They remember leaving Europe all those years ago when they were both very young, but not too young not to remember.

They remember crossing the Danube several times on their way from France. By the time they reached the salt-rich areas of Austria, they were quite grown; so grown, in fact, that, Eogan managed several times to sneak into the salt mines as a laborer.

"You were always such a rebel," Cath says, remembering him in his boots, a backpack strapped to his back, pickaxe in his hand, looking nothing like the son of a nobleman, which he was.

"I remember you being quite the rebel yourself," he says jokingly, recalling the last time he went down the salt mines, Cath in tow, disguised as a laborer herself.

But now they are here, on the Welsh plains, and life for the Celts is for the first time idyllic. There are no more wars, not even the battles for territory. They have taken possession of most of the plains, and nobody seems to bother them anymore. All their enemies seem to have evaporated into thin air, like the morning dew that often falls off the clovers.

"Do you want to talk about her," Eogan asks when he notices that Cath becomes distant, a longing look in her eyes?

"What is there to say, Eogan? She is gone, and nothing that I say will bring her back." Cath is hurt too at the loss of her mother, seemingly for no reason. It is this lack of reason that cuts her mostly. There is simply no explanation for why she is without a mother. It hurts her that her mother will not see her marry, or know any of her children. But she really doesn't have the words with which to explain to Eogan how she truly feels inside, not this time.

They remember, albeit, for different reasons, a time when they were about ten years old, and Cath was determined to dig up her mother's grave to retrieve her mirror. She remembered the stories of how her mother loved that mirror, and thought, at that tender age, that if she could just get it, hold it, it would somehow transfer upon her some of her mother's love.

Eogan remembers her frustration after her father found them, and reprimanded them for disturbing the grave. They hadn't even gotten half a foot down when Ailill discovered them, and carried a kicking and screaming Cath back home. But even Ailill understood where his daughter was coming from, despite her age. Eogan too understood; which is why he had agreed to help her in the first place.

But life on the Welsh Plains is everything that they dreamed and the Celts thrive. Even the moments of grief, when someone loved dies, are short. The grief is as fleeting as the summer, which proves to be very prosperous indeed.

The leaves on the trees start to turn and they know autumn is coming. They start the preparations for the winter long in advance, the community having grown substantially. The gods are really showing the Celts favor, and they appreciate it. They appreciate every blessing that they seem to be receiving in their new home.

"Autumn preparations are going well," Ailill tells Cath

on this particular afternoon. The air is starting to turn icy, and so they are both covered well.

"Yes, father; and the summer was very good," Cath says, mostly for reasons that she isn't comfortable discussing with her father, who still considers her to be his little girl.

They ride the length of the community, passing through farms that are busy preparing themselves for the coming winter months. One thing about life on the plains is that the winters are unforgiving. They are bitterly cold, and wet so that even the houses need to be prepared to take the knocks.

The autumn preparations come and go, everyone is ready for the winter now. The steel themselves against the elements, but it is a rather pleasant winter. It is cold. And it is wet. But they are so well prepared that the winter comes and goes without incident.

Everyone is happy, and it seems like nothing can upset their tranquility, and soon enough, the Celts are preparing for the festival of Beltaine again, ready, and oh so willing to offer up some of the treasures they have accumulated to Belenos.

But then the seers start to have dreams, waking visions of a bad time coming. They are not sure what to make of these, and so each one at first keeps his visions to himself, just until he is sure. The dreams, however, become more and more vivid, so that they have to consult with one another.

The Druids too start to have visions, of warfare, and battle, Celts falling to their left and their right. They cannot make out the army in the visions, not yet, but it is clearly a battle that the Celts lose. Troubled by these visions the Druids and seers now consult with one another, not sure still what this all means. But one thing is clear, they have to tell Ailill about the visions so that he can make the necessary preparations.

"There is a war coming, one that will not go well for us," Chief Druid starts immediately with the meat of the matter.

"What army?" Ailill asks, not sure how anyone would want to attack them when they have been living peacefully on the Welsh Plain, not bothering anyone.

"We don't know, yet. But the visions are clear, thousands of Celts will fall!" Chief Druid makes all of Ailill's fears suddenly seem very real.

"Why, why, why?" Ailill is anxious, and with the Celts not having fought in such a long time, rightly so.

"That is not clear just yet, but we think it's probably an army that we defeated in battle previously, come to exact revenge. Nothing is clear yet. But what we are sure of now, is that they are coming, soon!" The Chief Druid seldom sugarcoats anything with Ailill, both men expecting nothing but complete honesty from each other.

"Leave me..." Ailill is tormented suddenly with the thought of losing his people in a war that he did not start. The rules of battle have always been simple. What revenge is this that is suddenly sought against his people, a people who have been coexisting peacefully with everyone around them for so long?

The Druids leave him alone with the news that they have brought him. He is clearly troubled so that they don't expect him to offer up a solution immediately. They return to consulting with their various omens, fully aware that they should also be preparing for Beltaine. But how can they ask the gods for prosperity, when what they need now is protection?

There is a nervous tension in the air throughout the festivities, although only Ailill, the Druids, and the seers are aware of what is going on. Ailill is careful not to let the news get to anyone's ears just yet. He needs confirmation more solid than just the visions of some mystics. But they have never been wrong before, and although he hopes that this time they are, he knows that they aren't. He observes the festivities in as detached a fashion as he had done when Edain had died.

But then he receives distressing news from messengers posted at the edge of their territories. It's not news that he wants to hear, but it is delivered to him nonetheless. Two armies have set up camps around the border of the Celtic stronghold, one Greek, and one Roman, and they are obviously working together.

Ailill suddenly understands the nature of their predicament. It is not for land or territory; both armies have enough of that, their empires stretching vastly. They want to capture his people, embarrass them, make them slaves, and steal the one thing that the Celts have always been better at, their art, their skill with metals, and their knowledge. But why not just ask them for help, why a war, that will leave very many men dead, and their women slaves to these empires?

"I know why they've come. They want to steal our lifestyle. They want to crush us so that they can once more be seen as the centers of human endeavor and advancement. How can a people so civilized be so primitive in their thinking?" Ailill asks this of himself, not expecting the messengers to answer him. What answer could they give after all?

"We must fight, sir, fight for our lives. If it's a battle, they want, they will surely find one here." The messengers speak almost in unison, although a young man named Dunn does most of the talking.

"Yes, we will fight, if that is what they want. They dare

to bring a war to us; we will give them a battle they will never forget." Ailill sounds more confident than he is, remembering the Druid's words, 'a thousand Celts will fall at your left, a thousand at your right. The battlefield will flow with Celtic blood on that day!'

"We must inform the chieftains, get the generals ready," Dunn is excited at the prospect of a battle, aching to use his sword in real combat for the first time. He has always been a hothead, but one that deems himself skilled in the art of war. He speaks confidently, not knowing of course, what the Druids and seers have seen.

"No, wait. Not yet! We must bide our time carefully, and make sure first of the extent of the onslaught. Then we will inform everybody, and get them ready. The people are barely done celebrating Beltaine, and if we tell them of this now, it will seem to them that the gods have deserted us." Ailill instructs them to speak of this to no one and to return to their posts to keep an eye on the armies. If there is any movement, they should let him know. But it is clear that the war will come before the winter, perhaps in the autumn, when his people are busy with winter preparations.

He needs to think carefully about his next move; and how he can save as many of his people as he can. He has little concern for himself, but one person, in particular, occupies his mind. He has to make sure that he gets Cath to safety before the Greeks and Romans come. Hers will be a fate worse than death if she is captured by these barbarians.

CHAPTER 2

ALONE NOW IN HIS HOUSE, Cath riding with Eogan, and not with him for the first time in many moons, he wonders how he will get her to leave. She will not want to go, to leave her people. She is a Celtic princess, and she will, he knows, accept the weight of this responsibility. But he cannot imagine her in enemy hands.

His concern for his daughter is thick, shrouding around him like a cloak that he can't shake off. He is concerned for all his people. But mostly he is concerned for Cath. She cannot be captured. She will not be captured. But how can he convince her to leave? This bears heavily on him, more so than the two armies camped just beyond their borders, readier than they are, for the day of battle.

Ailill rides out alone, despite the setting sun. He has nothing to fear amongst his people. The threat lies in the distance, and it is a threat that he will have to do something about. But his concern for his daughter overrides his concern even for his people. He can't lose her too.

Everyone is still outside, enjoying the warmth left by the summer sun. They all look so happy, so content. He wonders what will become of his people when the armies come. He needs to devise a plan, a strategy for this warfare that will leave maximum casualties on his side of the battle lines. But from what he has been told by Dunn and his men the armies that have come to take from them the peace and prosperity they finally have here are formidable.

He deliberately avoids the river, knowing that Eogan will be there with Cath, even at this hour. She is safe with him. But how safe will she be, he wonders, in a few weeks, when the Romans and Greeks attack? They are ready for the battle, he knows this from reports. And they could attack at any time, even tonight. But he has to trust that these armies will follow the rules of engagement, and send an envoy to let the Celts know that they are about to be attacked. But the attack itself makes no sense to him, so he isn't sure if they will follow even this basic protocol.

The best time to attack would be in early autumn, Ailill thinks, when the weather is cooler unless of course the Greek and Roman armies are prepared for a showdown in the heat. He thinks that they are. They must be. Otherwise, why would they have set up camp already, and at the most strategic exit points if the Celts were to have any hope of escaping?

His mind races forward to the day of battle, and he has vivid images of the day, thanks to the Druids and seers. They need to consult with the gods, find out if they have done anything wrong to deserve this, and maybe, just maybe, thwart the attack. Ailill knows somehow that this won't help, the gods never really involving themselves in human affairs unless it is to receive praise and offerings.

From a hill, he looks out on the various homesteads. He is proud of what they have done here. And to lose it all now because of a few power-hungry soldiers, well that is a thought that doesn't sit well with him. He resolves in his head and heart to fight and to fall if need be, for this life they have built here. But he knows that he will fight better if he is assured of Cath's safety.

He knows what he needs to do, and he knows who will help him. As he rides home, he plays over the conversation that he must have with Eogan tomorrow. He can only hope that Cath will see reason, and retreat to the safety of Scotland, or Ireland. He takes this hope with him to bed.

"Let's go and talk outside," he says to Eogan when he arrives at his house the following morning. Eogan follows Ailill outside and around the side of the house. Since his marriage proposal to Cath, he has been very anxious to be alone with Ailill, who has the power to call off the marriage or put it on hold. He wonders what he has to say to him on this particular morning, so early.

"Do you love my daughter...Of course, you do!" Ailill answers his own question before Eogan does. But Eogan still feels the need to reassure him.

"I love her with everything that I am, sir!" Eogan's answer is passionate, a look of loving and longing hanging heavy in his eyes.

"I know son, I know. That is why this is so difficult for me. But you are the only person I think she will listen to." Ailill seems anxious now, and Eogan is worried. He senses that there is more to what Ailill is saying to him, and part of him, all of him, wishes that he would just come out with it.

Not really certain of where to start, Ailill decides to start at the beginning. He reminds himself constantly that he is not speaking to Eogan as one of the generals in his army. He is speaking to him, man to man, as a father would speak to the man who has promised to love his only child forever.

Eogan hangs on each word, waiting for the request to finally come out of Ailill's mouth. He knows what it is though, already, he thinks, but he needs to hear it. He knows that Ailill is about to ask him to send Cath away. But he also knows that he would never ask him to go with her. As a general in the army, his duty is first to his people. He would never desert them, never.

The conversation goes from one intense moment to the next and Ailill gets progressively anxious. He knows that he has been heard, but with no response from Eogan after a long while, he isn't sure what the young man is thinking. He has never been able to read Eogan, and this has frustrated him for a very long time. But he trusts his daughter's judgment, knowing that she is a remarkable judge of a man's character.

Eogan leaves without saying anything to Ailill, just the standard goodbyes. Ailill lets him go, understanding that he needs to process what is going on, and everything that might still happen.

In the meantime, news arrives that the armies on the edge of the Celtic territories are moving. And once again Ailill is anxious, knowing that there is little to no time to spare. If Cath is going to get out, she needs to get out now!

Cath has no way of avoiding the conversation, or her father much longer. Not that she doesn't try mind you, but eventually she just gives in to his looks, knowing that he needs to say what is on his mind. But when he starts, she is taken aback, not expecting the words that fall from her father's lips at all.

"This will not end well for us..." Ailill starts, knowing that beating about any sort of bush will not serve the situation. He remembers his conversation with Eogan, and he realizes that he just needs to ask Cath to get out now before the armies come. He eventually comes out with it. But like Eogan, Cath has no response to him, also needing to process what she has just heard.

Cath and her father discuss the battle and its possible outcomes, taking the conversation in a slightly different direction, but never straying too far from his request. Still, Cath doesn't answer what her father is actually asking of her. She is as skilled as he is in conversation, making her entire dialogue about her people.

"We've come so far father, and we've done so much here. What of the people, what will become of them?" she asks him, desperately searching him for answers that he simply does not have.

"I know, dear, I know. All this will be destroyed Cath, many men will fall, perhaps they all will. And you will be taken prisoner, kept as a trinket to the tyrants who've come to show us their strength. Still, I would fight better knowing that you are away from this all, away from danger, and away from the future, however short it will be, that I know you will have in the hands of these savages." Again Ailill tries to make her see reason; again he tries to convince her to leave. "You must get out now Cath, and get as far away from all of this as soon as possible."

"I can't leave father, I cannot desert my people, not now!" Cath speaks emphatically so that Ailill knows that anything that he says further on the matter will fall on deaf ears.

He watches her leave the room, seeing not the woman that is walking away from him, but seeing his little girl, skipping carefree, knowing that she will turn back. He almost expects her to turn around and come running towards him, jumping high on his hip, and kissing him full on his mouth. He remembers the red locks that framed the little girl's innocent face, her eyes big and far too bold on her face. But Cath is not a little girl anymore.

Cath escapes to the solitude of the cliffs and hills that are away from the main settlement. She doesn't know where the threat is, but she feels safer with the hills to overlook and protect her. She walks precariously close to the edge of the jagged cliffs and wonders at everything her father has just said. She thinks of the look in his eyes when he asked her to leave, knowing probably that she wouldn't.

She ponders the day of battle and thinks of all the possible outcomes. But she cannot accept that they will lose. She is not as prepared as her father seems to be, to accept that they will lose this battle. She will not accept this, no matter what the Druids and seers say, and no matter the size of the imposing army already camped out just beyond their borders. She just can't bring herself to accept this...

Cath starts to practice for the battle in secret. She leaves her home very early in the mornings, avoiding her father for many reasons, and she rides to the far edge of the settlement. After looking around to see that nobody has followed her, she takes out a slashing sword, a gift given to her by Eogan after he received a new one for his sixteenth birthday, and her daggers, her own personal collection. He holds the weapons in her hands, feeling the coolness of the steel, strangely loving it.

She does this every day, and with each day that passes, she feels her resolve to stay and fight to strengthen inside her. How can she, a princess, loved and adored by her people, leave them in their hour of need? The impossibility of this settles over her as the darkness reminds her that she needs to get home. By the time she is safely inside and locked behind the door to her bedroom, she is completely and utterly exhausted.

On this particular morning, Cath is more distracted than she should be. Her decision to stay hasn't changed, but she can't help but think of all the things that will happen to her at the hands of the Greeks and Romans. It is not even a matter of maybe. She knows that these evil men will have a string of punishments that they will not hesitate to enthusiastically meet out on her.

She hasn't noticed that she is being followed. After all, it is just before dawn, and she can't imagine that anybody else is awake, except for the farmers, of course. And why would they feel the need to follow her?

Eogan watches her warm-up and then settles almost immediately into practice. He watches as she moves, skillfully so, with the slashing swords in her hands. She moves like she is dancing, and Eogan is mesmerized. He finds himself moving closer and closer to her, until he is out in the open, and she can't help but to see him. She drops the swords.

"What are you doing here?" She isn't angry with him, almost as though she wanted him to catch her. But still, she is surprised.

"What are you doing here, Cath? You should be getting ready to leave!" Eogan speaks to her as if he knows of the conversation that Ailill had with his daughter.

"You've spoken with my father?!" As much a question as it is a statement, the beginnings of anger now stirring up inside her. But she manages to maintain her composure, to keep herself calm and measured.

"I have, and we both agree that it would be best if you..." Eogan stops himself mid-sentence, realizing that he is not doing a very good job of convincing Cath that leaving would be best for her. After all, she is fiercely independent, something which attracted him to her in the first place. So making her feel like a weak woman who needs to be saved now, who needs to run away, is probably not the best way to approach this situation.

One thing is clear, Cath will not leave. Eogan just watches her for a while, taking in the details of the woman that he loves. She is a myriad of contradictions. The most obvious is how delicate she appears, yet he knows that she is anything but. He knows her ability with a sword, and even with daggers. He knows that she is a very capable rider too, more so even than many men in the settlement.

After watching her a little longer he decides to leave her alone, knowing that at least she has heard everything that he has to say. Eogan decides that the best thing to do is to leave Cath with the opportunity to reflect on what she has just heard and to think about his request. He hopes that she will see reason. He prays that she will see reason and leave before they are attacked.

Cath does have a lot to think about. She shifts from thoughts of their life here, and thoughts of how she might get away. This seems impossible anyway if they're already surrounded, but she can't help the thoughts that creep up on her. But she shakes them from her; she doesn't even want to be tempted in the least to leave. She goes through the million scenarios in her head, and for every reason why she should leave, she manages to find a reason for her to stay.

After hiding her swords and daggers she goes for a ride alone. The sun has set completely now, but the moon is high in the sky so that the path in front of her is clear. She can see quite far out ahead of her in fact, and even the smoke coming through the chimneys is clearly visible. The peace and quiet, the calm of the scene in front of her belie the threat that is just beyond the threshold of their borders.

She gets to one of the streams coming off the river that

rages in the distance, her meeting place with Eogan, and she brings her horse to a halt. She suddenly can't hold back the tears that flow from her eyes, so she cannot proceed. She gets off the horse and goes to the water's edge, throwing some of it on her face. The water mixes with her tears and they stream steadily down her face. She sits on the earth now and just lets it all out.

The thought that she might not be able to marry, to live happily ever after, is uppermost in her mind. This, along with the thoughts of what could or couldn't happen when the armies come fill her head like clouds of smoke that seem to want to come out of her ears. But there is just no escaping these thoughts, not a single one.

Meanwhile, Ailill paces the length and breadth of his house. He has concerns of his own, concerns for his people, and concerns for his daughter. He has no idea what to do, but he knows that he will have to decide very soon. He needs to clear his head.

He decides to go for a ride, without checking that Cath is back yet. He will avoid riding the route that they always take so that he can minimize the chance of bumping into her. If he did, what would he have to say to her? All he wants is for her to leave this place and get to safety, but he has run out of ways to ask her.

He rides to a nearby grove and settles his horse down under the trees. The moon really is bright tonight, and Ailill can make out every outline of the little homesteads in the settlement. There are many of them, but none of them is so close to one another so as to impose on each other.

Ailill breathes in the night air and lets the smell of everything around him overwhelm him. The mixture of burning wood and coal, and the crispness of the landscape come up into his nostrils and he almost holds his breath.

They cannot lose everything that they have managed to build here. But what can he do to avoid the massive carnage that he's been told is coming? He rides back home just before the sun comes up, not realizing that he's been out for so long. But he gets home just before the first light makes its way over the horizon, and goes straight to bed after checking that Cath is safe and sound in her bed.

Cath too has many thoughts going through her head, so that it is difficult for her to sleep. She has long left the house, her bed covers wrapped tightly around her other bed coverings, so that it is just enough to fool Ailill, who would never come into her bedroom uninvited, just peeping around the door to check that she is still in bed.

But Cath is not in bed. She is away from the settlement in her secluded battling arena, practicing for the coming war. She is more determined than ever to take down as many soldiers as possible before the Greeks and Romans take her. And she knows that she will, as she slashes her sword out in front of her. She knows that the steel of her blade will pierce many men before she finally succumbs to exhaustion, or before a blade pierces her side and she falls to the ground.

CHAPTER 3

AILILL HAS to meet with the Druids and seers again. He needs clarity on this situation, and he needs to find out if anything has changed since last they spoke. There is an urgency that overcomes him now, and he knows that time is fast running out for his people, and for his daughter.

The seers set about divining, trying to see as far into the future as possible. They try to see the specifics of the coming battle, try to see who will win, and who, if anybody, will survive. It all starts out as a haze, smoke everywhere, and they are unable to see through the white. But then it becomes clear, and they become increasingly anxious.

How do they tell Ailill that nothing has changed? How do they tell him that they still see the fall of the Celtic people and that many men will fall on the day of battle? They really have no words to even begin to articulate the carnage that they see. So they look to the Druids for the words.

The Druids see the same thing that the seers do. They even see more detail, and it is this detail that the Chief

Druid cannot keep from Ailill. He takes him outside, leaving the seers consulting with the gods trying to make sense of everything. The Chief Druid has Ailill by the arm, practically pulling him away from the house, almost as though he doesn't want anybody to hear what he has to say.

"Have you spoken to Cath about...things?" The Druid gets straight into it, as usual, and this is appreciated by Ailill. He also appreciates that he doesn't have this conversation in front of everyone else, knowing that this would be better for Cath.

"She will not leave!" Ailill is emphatic in his response but leaves it hanging in the air almost as though the man in front of him will offer up a suggestion, or even a potion that will have Cath disappear from the impending madness. But there is nothing but silence between them for the longest time, both men caught up with imaginings of what lies ahead.

"I thought she wouldn't," the older man finally says. He has known Cath her whole life, and he knows the commitment she has to her people. But this commitment has only ever been expressed in times of peace. Now, with a war coming, the true test of her character is being revealed. And it is a test that Cath is obviously determined to pass.

But the odds are stacked high against the Celts. They have a formidable army, yes, but one that has not seen war in many moons. And practicing for war doesn't sharpen one's skills as actual warfare. The Greeks and Romans seem to be all too aware of this.

But still, they are taking no chances it seems. The combined strength of both armies will be formidable on the day of battle. And they seem to have grown in strength and skill. Reports from Dunn and his men are not promising, and even now, with summer still full in the air, these armies are practicing for the day that they will bring the Celts down. And this day seems to be closer at hand with each sleepless night that Ailill has.

But Ailill is not the only one having sleepless nights. Cath is caught in the throes of a nightmare so vivid, that she can smell the blood pouring from the wounded Celts. In her dream, she walks the full length of the battlefield, seemingly invisible to the attacking armies. But her people are not invisible, and they are taking serious blows from these barbarians. Cath cannot believe her eyes, and as she goes to move a little girl out of the path of a Roman sword, she starts awake.

She is wet with sweat, dripping from her forehead and her chest. She cannot feel her hands, wrapped tightly in the bedclothes, sweaty and white, so tight is her grip on the sheets. Cath looks around, seeing that she is in the safety of her bedroom, but still so consumed by fear and trauma that she may as well be outside, vulnerable to the enemy who is hungry for her blood. Her blood, she whispers to herself in the dark. And suddenly a thought starts to fill her head, uninvited.

She wonders if the Greeks and Romans will not be satisfied with just her. She is after all the pride of the Celts, of royal blood. Will her blood not be a fair trade for the blood of her people? She knows that she will be a valuable prisoner, dead or alive. But she knows too that they would not have come with an army 300,000 strong if she was all they wanted. They have come to completely destroy her people.

Cath becomes increasingly reserved. She avoids her father, and she avoids Eogan. Both men don't know what to do about this, but they have to focus their energies on the battle now. They have got to just trust that soon enough, and sooner rather than later, Cath will see reason, and get to safety while there still exists a window of opportunity.

But with every day that passes, Cath gives no indication that she is planning on going anywhere, and summer is fast coming to an end. The people are also starting to get ready for the autumn preparations. And why wouldn't they, since they know nothing of the danger that is now practically on their doorsteps?

Still, she practices, even though her faith is waning. She catches her father in conversation with his generals often, and he seems to grow increasingly despondent. This feeling seems to be seeping into her veins too now, and she is losing hope. But she is determined not to go without a fight. If her people will fall, then she will fall with them or be captured while fighting with them, and fighting for them.

Eogan too is distracted by the thought of losing this war. He no longer questions the reasons for it mind you, knowing just that the enemy has come. And while he too has started his own preparations for the battle, he knows in his heart that they are nowhere near ready to face the Greeks and Romans.

But one thing that he is determined to do is not to let his concern show on his face. He knows that his regimen trusts him for guidance. They are looking to him for hope, hope that isn't there. But he offers them this hope nonetheless, making sure that at every practice session, he reminds the soldiers under his command not to say anything of the war to anyone who does not need to know about it. Not yet, anyway.

Cath arrives home after her own training session to find

Ailill waiting for her. They look at each other for a long time, unspoken words falling from their lips and hanging between them like pieces of cloth on a tree. They know what the other is thinking. They know what the other wants to say, but they cannot, for the longest time, bring themselves to say it.

But then Ailill starts, pouring out the words that are heavy on his heart. He must make her see reason, and he must make her understand that hers is a sacrifice that she need not make. She must get away from this place that now seems so wretched, this beautiful place that has come to feel like a prison to him. If nothing else, then she will be able to get away and tell their story, regaling the success story that was their life before the armies came.

"You have got to live to tell the story of what we have done here Cath, you just must!" Ailill entreats her, trying a different angle that he hopes will work this time.

"Why me, father? Why must I be the one to get away, why not someone else? What story will be told of me, if I run now?"

"You will not be running Cath, don't think of it like that. The truth is, I will fight better if I know that you are safe. I will fight so that I can see you again, Eogan too. You must do this Cath, if not for yourself, then for us. How can we go into a losing battle with you on our minds? You have to see that this will be a burden that neither of us can carry!" He jumps between reasons, pulling on every reason that he can think of for his daughter to getaway.

After a long silence, and Ailill repeating himself far too many times, Cath relents. She promises to think about it, but cannot at the moment guarantee that she will change her mind. She still can't imagine herself leaving her people, not now, not when they finally need her the most. She needs to show them that she truly deserves the honor of being called a Celtic princess, and she is determined to be more than a princess by name only.

But Ailill and Eogan are determined to make one more attempt to get Cath out. The problem that both men have is that they cannot even focus fully on their training with the thought of Cath in the back of their minds. They decide to corner her together and present a united front. Perhaps if she sees them together, she will realize, once and for all, the urgency of the situation, and leave.

Cath looks from her father to Eogan, who now speak over one another, no longer concerned for the nature of their own relationship. Both men have a common goal; they are one in purpose. It would have been amusing to her if the conversation wasn't so serious, and so she just takes in everything that both men are saying.

She takes it all in, word for word, and allows the single request that both men are making to settle over her. There comes a moment in the interaction when she sees the point that they are making, and she has no choice but to accept that perhaps they are right.

Perhaps, just perhaps, if she removes herself from the equation, then her father and Eogan will fight better. Maybe they will be more determined to win the war since this will ensure that they get to see her again. She must admit to herself that it will be near impossible for them to rescue her if they survive, and it will therefore be easier for them to be reunited if she is safely away from the thick of things.

She takes a moment to let the finality of her decision to sink in, but both men can see that she has finally seen reason. They are both ecstatic but don't show it. The last thing that Cath needs now is a show of excitement, not with the burden of the choice that she has had to make so heavy.

She leaves the two of them in silence, and they remain silent long after she has gone. Ailill and Eogan are unable to even look at each other now, knowing that they have essentially banished Cath from the settlement, albeit for her own good. But feelings of guilt stir in both of them so that they are not even able to say goodbye to one another.

Cath doesn't speak to either of them for the next two days. She is preoccupied with what she must take with her, what remnants of a culture and a people she can carry with her safely, proof that they once were. But she can think of nothing so that by the time she is ready to leave, the only thing that she has with her are six little daggers and a backpack. She leaves Eogan's sword on her bed.

She hopes that he will use it in battle and that he will bring many Greeks and Romans down before he falls. Cath doesn't dwell too long on her love falling, or her father even. She has to keep alive the hope that is in her heart, despite the facts that keep surfacing to the top of her mind.

Cath gets going soon before the sun comes up before anybody has stirred in the settlement. She cannot bring herself to say goodbye to anybody, not even to her friends, and so she steals away like a thief in the night. There is a small gap between the armies camped out on the outskirts of the settlement, and Cath steals through this gap. She looks at the many tents in awe, and she cannot believe the size of this army that has come to take from her people the peace that they have managed to build on the Welsh plains.

By the time the sun comes out, she has cleared the armies, despite the slowness of her pace. She knows the land well, and as light, as she is traveling, it would be difficult for even the most skilled Greek or Roman spotter to see her. She trudges on, her mind filling with many scenarios, her eyes filling with tears, and her heart heavy.

She really does not want to go. But she knows exactly where her father and Eogan are coming from. She gets that they fear her, and she understands why. She knows that they will fight better in her absence and that without the burden of her safety weighing on them, they will both be unstoppable in battle. But still, she hates the fact that she is now moving further and further away from the only home that she has known for a very long time.

After summiting one of the many hills around her home, she looks back on the plains as they start to turn the colors of autumn. It's too soon for this change, and Cath isn't sure if she is just imagining things, but still, the whole land looks strangely barren. She closes her eyes and then opens them again, just to make sure that she is in fact seeing what she is.

She looks at the Greek and Roman camps, spread almost as wide as the settlement, and it finally registers with her that this war will not end well for the Celts. From her perch, she can make out the soldiers stirring from their tents, already preparing for battle. They are obviously hungry for Celtic blood, and they will stop at nothing until the last Celtic warrior has fallen.

Cath sits on the edge of a precipice, knowing that they can't, even if they wanted to, see her now. She imagines her father stirring and checking on her. She imagines that Eogan will go to the place where he caught her practicing for the battle she will now not fight. She wonders what will go through their minds when they find that she has left. Will they be relieved? Or will they be disappointed that she did not give them a chance to say goodbye?

But how could she? How could she bid farewell to the

two men that have been her everything for the longest time? How can she be expected to listen to them mocking her with promises of seeing each other soon, when it is clear that they will not? Does her father even know the extent of the armies that have come to attack them, she wonders?

With all these thoughts running through her head she starts to second guess her decision. She thinks about how she might get back past the soldiers who seem to have narrowed the gap now, the settlement completely enclosed. She knows though that she understands the lay of the land sufficiently to get past them without them noticing her. But she thinks better of it.

Yes, she has gotten out, and yes, she is moving away from her people. But that doesn't mean that she must go too far. She decides to head out towards Scotland as directed by her father, where she will be able to survive off the land, living like a nomad. But she will not stray too far so that she can be close enough to join the battle when it starts, and by the time she gets involved in the war, it will be too late for her father or Eogan to do anything about it.

In fact, she thinks, she will be able to sneak onto the battlefield once they've started fighting, and that her father and Eogan will be so busy battling that they might not even notice that she is amongst them. Cath breathes in, deeply, and lets the air fill her chest. She breathes in her home, and then exhales, letting herself and her people go, for now, but knowing that she will be back!

She just has to be back, and she just needs to be involved in the battle. She knows that her father will not be pleased, and neither will, Eogan, but that is not something that she can worry too much about right now. She chooses her path carefully, and heads out, albeit more slowly, in the direction of Scotland.

The road is tough, the terrain rough, but she manages it well. She has ridden these paths many times before, with and without her father, with and without Eogan. So she is well versed in the lay of the land. She moves almost too effortlessly across the hills, and past the various plateaus. She has to stop herself as she moves though, especially when she realizes that she moves too quickly.

The shifting landscape intrigues her as she gets further and further from her home. She reaches a part of the land that she has not traveled before, at least not as an adult, and she has to stop to get her bearings. She looks around, from left to right, and then around. She is not confused, just wondering which way would be best for her to go.

But then she chooses a path and is on her way again. She makes for Scotland, at least in the direction thereof, and she feels even more overwhelmed. She is not overwhelmed by her journey; the journey that lies ahead of her, but by the path that she has come. She is moving far too quickly, and this bothers her. She really does not want to get too far from her home too quickly.

She continues pressing on, however, despite her reservations, and her desire to just turn back. She questions herself often, questioning her resolve to leave, and her resolve to stay. She thinks that she should have stayed and that she should have let her father and Eogan just deal with the repercussions of her staying.

But then again, she remembers all the things that they said to her, and she thinks of the look on their faces when they said it, and then she thinks that maybe she made the right decision. But how could she leave her people at this critical time in their existence, when it seems that they are about to be annihilated?

Still, she moves on and gets even further away from the

settlement than she was. But she can't help it. Each step brings her further and further from her people, but each step also takes her further from danger, and she can't deny the sense of relief that has overcome her suddenly. But she is determined to get back!

CHAPTER 4

IT TAKES a while for Ailill to accept that his daughter has left, but at least she has. But that she did not even say goodbye to him hurts him more than the pending war allows him to process. There is no time for him to entertain what he is feeling. He needs to strategize for the battle that is coming.

Eogan too is troubled by Cath's sudden disappearance. But he knows that at least now she is safe. Both he and Ailill have confidence in Cath's ability to survive out there. She has always been more at home outdoors than she ever was in her home. He can also confidently now begin to strategize for the battle.

They still have not told anybody who does not need to know about the danger. They cannot risk panic, and everyone trying to get out, which would just lead to premature slaughter. But there is an increased military feel in the settlement, one that has everyone asking questions. Ailill manages to get them calm by saying that they are preparing for a fair, one that will see the armies, under all the generals, performing for the people. In the absence of real warfare, what better use can he think of for his soldiers, after all?

But even as he says this to his people, those who ask him of course, he believes himself less and less. What else can he say though that will not incite panic? He knows though that he will have to let the people know what is happening soon enough. He would rather it were later than sooner, however.

Cath's mind too is occupied with thoughts of home. Even as she travels further and further from her home, she finds herself thinking of her father. She wonders if he has perhaps told the people, yet of what waits for them just beyond the horizon, she wonders too if they have started preparing for the war. She also wonders what his strategy is going to be for winning the war, knowing her father, and knowing that no matter what the Druids say, Ailill will not go out without a fight.

She thinks too of Eogan, the man she was supposed to spend the rest of her life with. She wonders too at his preparations for the war, knowing that he is skilled in battle, but also knowing that he has never in his life been on an actual battlefield. This thought bothers her most of all, that her people, for the most part, are so inexperienced in actual warfare. The mock fighting at the games on their days of sport is one thing. But to be caught in actual battle is another thing altogether.

Meanwhile, the Greeks and Romans solidify their own strategy. They practice new formations, formations that they have never used in battle before so that they know this will catch the Celts quite by surprise. And they are ready; so ready, in fact, that they are already confident of a win before even a single horse has made it on to the field of battle.

They obviously have a plan. And it is clearly well

thought out. No matter how the Celts respond to the onslaught, it is clear that many of them will fall. It is clear who the winners will be. And this belief in a clear victory spurs them on.

The Celtic chiefs gather for another meeting. The time has come for them to let the people know what is going on. With reports of the Greek and Roman preparations becoming more and more urgent, there is no time for them to continue the farce. Nobody will be able to leave the settlement anyway, now, so they need to get the people as prepared as they can for the day of battle.

But before they do, they consult with their oracles for the last time. Ailill hopes beyond hope that perhaps the forecast will have changed. It's been just a few days since he consulted with the Druids, who painted an even bleaker picture than before, but he still hopes that the oracles will have had a different premonition.

But all they get from these old men is guidance. They offer no hope, nothing to give them any sort of indication that things might turn out better for the Celts. Instead, they tell Ailill and his chiefs what they already know. And they instruct him on the best way to approach this battle so that there are at least a few survivors who will tell the world the story of what happened here.

But Ailill knows all this. He knows that if the Romans follow the protocol of battle, there will be some people left to tell their story. This is not a show of compassion mind you. The winners of any war need to leave survivors who will tell of their victory from the perspective of the losers, stroking their already inflated egos.

Ailill barely has a moment alone now. The chiefs and generals surround him constantly, looking to him for instruction. They need him now, more than ever before, to show leadership. And he is up to the task, pulling all his reserves of energy and his experience with warfare to the fore. He has to fight now, and he has to fight hard if he is to have any hope of being reunited with his daughter. But even if he never sees Cath again, at least now he is sure that she has a fighting chance.

The armies have now started to move. Advancing ever closer towards the Celtic settlement. Dunn's messengers get news of this movement to Ailill, who relays this message to his generals. He is in a full military mode now, and he even walks around with his slashing swords in his pouches, and his daggers parked in his belt. He is as prepared as he is going to be for the attack, more so than most of the men under him. But some of his generals, all except two, in fact, have also had real-world war experiences. And it is time for him to call on this experience.

"The armies are advancing, and they will attack within the month, I fear. All we can do now is to be as prepared as we can be for the attack and to try and keep as many people safe as possible. Life under Roman or Greek rule will be no life at all, and even the hardest amongst us won't survive this." He lets them know what they are fighting for, and against. Ailill hopes that this will be enough to spur them on and to get them ready for the day of battle.

Cath is also just a few days' ride away from her home now, and she has a bad feeling. The armies closing in on her people have disappeared over the horizon now so that all she sees is a shimmer of steel in the distance. But what she knows is that there are many of them, too many. And even if she makes it back in time to help her people with the war, all she will manage to do is to bring a few of the attacking soldiers down before she herself is taken. But the whole situation is hopeless now, she fears, and for the first time, she fully understands what her father and Eogan were so fearful of.

She presses on though, in the direction of Scotland. If only her people had settled in this area, they might have had a better chance of winning the war. The country is surrounded by hills, lush forests, moors, and lochs, so battle on horseback is difficult. She knows that her people are skilled riders, but not as skilled as the Romans. Even the Greeks, with their leisurely ways, are formidable on horseback.

Her horse is tired now, and so is she. She must rest for the night, and chooses a spot near a loch, under the protection of the trees. She does not realize how tired she actually is from all her thinking and traveling, and soon enough, she is asleep under the illusionary safety of the night.

But her sleep isn't peaceful. She tosses and turns in the fallen leaves that she has gathered to make a bed so that soon enough she is on the muddy earth. She doesn't stir awake. The thoughts in her head are anything but peaceful, though. It is impossible for her to escape from them.

Once again, she is on the field of battle. And once again she is surrounded by death. She sees her friends falling in droves, but she is unable to help. It is as if she is a ghost amidst the people battling, seen by nobody, felt by nobody. All she can do is watch the carnage as it plays out around her.

Cath catches her father in the distance. And for a moment, it seems as though she sees him too. She mouths his name, but no sound comes out of her mouth. In a split second, her father looks away from her, and he is caught between four Romans. He fights valiantly, and the Romans all fall. Cath can feel her smile growing as it seems that her father has the upper hand over his attackers.

But then she watches in horror as two blades pierce through his stomach from the back. She tries to scream for him as blood comes out of his mouth. The red seems excessive as it pours out of his mouth and nose and then starts to spray out of his ears. She must get to him to stop the bleeding.

But she can't. As she tries to move toward him it seems to her that she is going backward instead. She feels like her feet have become heavy like they are stuck in the mud, but there is just no way for her to take even a single step toward the man who gave her life.

If only she could get to him. If only she could hold him in her arms in his final moments, and tell him that everything is going to be fine. But she just can't get to him. And as he falls to the ground Cath feels the life drain from her too. She tries to turn away from the picture in front of her. But just as she does, she wishes almost immediately that she hadn't.

What she sees next is just as grueling, as painful. She is now face to face with Eogan. And in the split second that their eyes meet, she watches in horror as his head is removed from his body in one neat stroke from a blade, the handler of which she can't see. She reaches for him, but again, she seems to be moving away from him, and she just has to watch as his head separates from his body and falls to the ground.

Cath feels suddenly that she is consumed by flames. Red and orange and blue surround her completely and envelope her. But she feels nothing. All she can do is to look on in anguish as every last Celt on the battlefield, man, woman, and a child die. The horror of it all is just too much for her.

She starts awake. She looks around for her father, and

for Eogan, but they are not here. She is alone and she is afraid. She looks at herself, for any signs of burning, but there is nothing. But she is wet with sweat, dripping so that the water escaping from her mixes with the water on the ground.

Cath feels for where her weapons are, and she looks around for any danger. But there is nothing around here except for the animals that are just stirring from their lairs. There is no danger here, except for the danger in her mind. But it feels very real, and she has to find a way to shake the feeling at the bottom of her stomach.

With the first light of dawn, she throws herself into the loch, as much to clean up as to rid herself of the sense of foreboding that she has. But this feeling will not leave her. It will go nowhere so that she knows that she has to deal with it.

She walks beside her horse now, not wanting to get much further from home than she has already gone. Every part of her is telling her to turn back so that she can fight and fall with her people. But she senses that it is still too soon. She travels in the same circle twice, another attempt at not creating too much distance between herself and her home.

Cath must come up with a plan, and quickly. But what, she asks herself. How can she, alone, bring down the large army that is quickly moving in on her people? What can she possibly do to save her people?

Her mind is consumed with coming up with a plan. So consumed is she in fact, with her new chain of thinking that she doesn't even realize how far she has gone. She is just traveling, side by side with her trusted steed, totally unaware of the ground she is covering.

By nighttime, she still has no plan, and she is well and

truly in Scotland now. Still no sign of human life around her at all, she comes upon a hillock. She settles beside it, and takes out her provisions, some nuts and berries left. She puts them into her mouth slowly, determined that she will not be sick; although she cannot remember the last time she ate.

After the last berry has disappeared from her sack, she settles down to rest. But how can she, when her mind is so occupied? She is determined that she will think of something that will rescue her people. But the more she tries to force her mind to focus, the deeper she goes into a haze. Nothing makes sense to her at all anymore.

She tries to call on the gods but stumbles on her words. Cath tries to shake the words out of her, but it does not help. Her thoughts seem to merge and fuse with one another so that nothing in her head makes any sort of sense. She tries to close her eyes before she realizes that they're already closed. Why is she suddenly feeling so disoriented?

Cath gets up and tries to walk around for a bit, trying to shake the feeling of confusion off her. But she simply cannot. She sits back down with her eyes closed and she holds on to her horse's reins, just so that she does not lose it. She also needs to feel that there is at least some semblance of reality left around her, everything feeling like a dream suddenly.

When she opens her eyes, she is almost blinded by the light. But from where, since it was just night. Could she have fallen asleep? And if so, is she now not still sleeping? And where is her horse? It takes her a moment to adjust to the piercing white light, and when she does, she sees that she isn't too far off from a grove. Perhaps her horse has wandered into it, between the trees.

She can't shake the feeling of confusion though, but

everything around her is as clear as crystal. She heads out towards the grove and feels a breeze brush across her face and through her hair. It feels like she is being kissed gently by the wind, caressed by the sun. Amidst her confusion, she cannot shake the sudden feeling of pure bliss.

She searches for the horse, but she can't find it. She notices that the trees are stronger than the ones on the Welsh plain, with thicker trunks. She has to reach out and touch one of them, just to make sure that what she is seeing actually is. The bark of the trees is tender to the touch, yet sturdy.

Cath watches as a leaf falls from the tree, and then another. Suddenly, as though caught up in a gust, many leaves start to fall towards her and circle her. She is suddenly enveloped in a whirlwind of leaves, so that the only thing she sees is green and brown, fusing together until all she sees is gold. Again she gets the sense that she is dreaming, but how can she be, when she can actually feel the leaves on her face?

The leaves suddenly settle, flowing to the ground almost in slow motion. Cath looks around her now, once again seeing everything around her as clear as crystal. She is still in the grove. It is the same grove, except that everything around her suddenly has a shimmer. It looks as though the trees have been plated in bronze, silver, and gold. It's beautiful. But it's also unreal, very surreal.

Cath looks around her in wonder. What is this place that she has stumbled on, this place that she now finds herself in? She can't help but touch everything she sees, the trees, the leaves on the trees, the grass, and even the earth seems to be embedded with precious gems. She looks at everything around her in absolute amazement.

Then she spots movement in the trees. Her hand is

quick on the place where her daggers were, and they're not there. She hides behind a tree, amazed again by how broad the trunk is. She has to peep around the broad base of the tree, and strain to see what could be causing the commotion. She sees nothing.

There is a sudden movement in the tree that she is under, and she tries to get to another tree. But just then she spots afoot, which disappears quickly into the leaves. It is a delicate foot, from what she can make out, a young girl's foot. But now it is gone, and the tree is once again still, save for the leaves that are blowing gently in the breeze.

She doesn't know if she has been seen, but she thinks she must have been, but by whom? Who is this young woman, or this little girl, that moves so effortlessly in the trees? Cath strains to see, but the tree has gone dead still now. She cannot see anything except for the green leaves that look like they've just woken for spring.

What place is this?

She looks around in wonder at everything that she sees. A million questions fill her head, but the answers seem to be far off in the distance. How is it that everything around her seems so real and yet it doesn't at the same time? All at once, she feels like she is caught in a dream and that she doesn't even want to wake up yet.

Awe overcomes her as she continues to look at the detail around her. Everything seems to have taken on a magical feel, one that she cannot, will not escape. She feels like she should not be here, but here she is, stuck almost in this waking dream. What is going on around her, she wanders again?

She looks at all the leaves around her, coming up off the ground again and then settling back on the earth. She is caught in sheer wonderment, looking at every single one of these leaves, it seems, all at the same time, as they rise and fall individually. Cath cannot help but shake her head again, as though she were trying to get water out of her ears after a dip in the nearby lake.

Where is she, she wonders, again!

CHAPTER 5

CATH HAS HEARD of a place like this before, long ago as a child. She remembers it now like it was yesterday. It's as though her mother is telling her the story. But how can this be, when she doesn't even remember her mother's voice? Or does she?

She looks to the hills in the distance, through the trees. Incredibly, they seem to change their shape the longer she looks at them. Now they are hills, then they are mountains, and then they give way to groves and forests. She must have a closer look.

As she walks in the direction of these shape-shifters, the trees around here seem to whisper in the breeze. The warm air kisses the side of her face gently, and she feels strangely safe in this place. She also feels completely exposed and vulnerable, but not at all in a bad way. She finds herself getting inexplicably emotional, like a sense of relief has suddenly overcome her. But why would she feel so relieved in this weird place?

But it is truly beautiful. Everything seems to speak to her in this place, the flowers, trees, and even the grass seems to be whispering to her. But she cannot make out what they are saying to her, or if they are even speaking to her.

She looks around for people, hoping that she can spot the girl whose foot she saw in the trees. It has been days since she has spoken to anyone really, and she just needs someone other than herself to talk to. She just needs to see one other person so that she doesn't feel like she is losing her mind.

The hills have changed shape again, and now the trees seem to go on forever. She has to stop, and question herself. Is she losing her mind? Is this all an illusion? She can't be sure; everything just seems so very real.

She comes across low-hanging fruit in a tree, and then she sees the same fruit hanging from the bushes nearby. Now she is sure that she has lost her mind. She is sure that she must have eaten something bad on her journey, perhaps something poisonous. But she knows the country so well. She knows what to eat and what to avoid. Her father went to great lengths to school her in such matters. How could she have made a mistake?

Reaching for a fruit she is suddenly taken aback by its appearance. What once appeared to her as red is now a golden hue; much like the carvings, she has seen decorating ornaments back home. Then again, it appears to be a delicious red color, so she cannot resist picking it.

She looks it over in her hands. And just as it becomes golden again, she brings it to her mouth and takes a small bite. She lets the flavor settle on her tongue, and then she chews carefully on it. Her mouth explodes with the feeling of apples and oranges and fruits that she has never tasted and before she can stop herself, she is swallowing. The feeling overwhelms her absolutely.

It is quite an experience. Not quite a taste, but a feeling, or feelings, and she is almost knocked to the ground. Cath looks around to check that nobody is watching her as she feels her face broaden into the biggest smile. She can't help herself. She just feels completely and utterly like a little girl again, tasting a sweet cake for the first time.

She moves around this strange place, still unsure if she will allow herself to believe that she is where she thinks she is. Where she knows she is. But how could she be, a human being in the Otherworld, how can this be? She needs to be sure. If only she can see the young girl from earlier again, to get confirmation that she is where she thinks she is.

The landscape becomes more beautiful as she continues her exploration of the Otherworld. She notices things just before they disappear, only to be replaced by more beautiful things, but nothing that she can talk with, nothing to give her absolute confirmation. She continues to search for it though.

She hears a strange buzzing sound that seems to be coming from all around her. She looks up, and then from side to side. Still, she sees nothing, even though the sound of the buzzing seems to be getting closer. She thwarts these imaginary creatures from her face, creatures that are not there. Or at least she hasn't seen them yet.

Then suddenly and without warning, she is surrounded by what looks like a million little birds, beating their wings so rapidly that you cannot even make out the outline of them. They buzz and hum like hornets, but they are definitely not hornets. They are beautiful multi-colored birds. Tiny yes, but birds all the same.

Cath watches them as they move in front of her and then around her. She is mesmerized so that she is unable even to move. Her eyes just follow the delicate formations of the tiny flying creatures in front of her. They move away from her and towards her, seemingly at the same time, and then they split into groups, two groups, and then six groups, and then ten. It's quite a spectacle to behold.

When she finally regains her composure she realizes that she is not even breathing. She inhales, and then practically gasps out. Then she takes short, shallow breaths, although she feels like she needs to breathe deeply. But she can't. She just stands there with her mouth wide open, breathing very fast. Then suddenly they are gone.

The silence seems to intrude on her now, in the absence of the humming. Cath looks around her, searching for the tiny creatures that were just here, but are now gone. She lets out a sigh now and then manages at last to slow her breathing. She is suddenly filled with incredible excitement.

She moves around more determinedly now. She looks behind every tree that she passes, around every bush, in every hole. With the changing scenery, her eyes finally make the adjustment. Not that the scenery stops changing mind you, but she simply takes it all in, enjoying it all.

Cath isn't sure if she has been spotted or not, but if she has, then nobody seems very interested in her. She is after all, in the domain of the gods now, so why would they see her as any sort of threat? But she does question how it is that she ended up here. What threshold could she have crossed, and when? And how does she go back over to the other side?

Panic quickly sets in. But as quickly as she starts to panic, she starts to form the plan that she has been waiting for. She remembers the battle that is about to go down and the prophecies of the Druids and the seers. If she can just speak to the gods on behalf of her people, then maybe, just maybe!

But where are the gods? How is it that she has seen

nobody thus far? Well, except for the foot that she saw in the trees. But whose foot was it? It can't have been a god, she thinks, since the foot and its owner disappeared at the mere sight of her. She is a little confused by this, but still, she presses on, determined to see a god.

No sooner has the thought fully formed in Cath's mind, when she sees a group of ethereal-looking girls running across a meadow that she is certain wasn't there before. They are all barefoot, and tiny so Cath knows that the foot, she saw belonged to one of them.

Cath follows these little nymphs, keeping a decent distance between her and them, which isn't difficult since the women in front of her seem to be determined to get to where they're going. Soon enough they are in another grove, as beautiful as the first one, as majestic. The trees look like they are embedded with jewels so that Cath runs her fingers across the barks just to be sure. It seems like a very elaborate illusion because as soon as her fingers touch the wood, all she feels is the wood, tender and sturdy all at once.

They come upon a clearing, very elaborately decorated. And the scene that opens up in front of her has her shrink back, not in fear, but in sheer amazement. She sees the nymphs join a group of men who can only be described as beautiful. They take their hands and skip around in an almost dance, then they are separated. Cath watches this closely, curious as to what is going on.

But then the nymphs are taken by the men into various tents and canopies, where the nymphs attend to their every whim. The scene grows, as more men and some women join in, taking their places around the festive setup. These newcomers are attended to by more nymphs so that Cath is aware of the status of these people. She wonders how it is that humans are attended to by nymphs in the Otherworld.

Upon closer inspection, however, she notices that the people being attended to by the nymphs have got intricate markings on their arms, some on their backs, and some of the men are marked on their chests. She gets as close as she can without being seen, just to get a closer look at these markings. The markings also seem to shift in shape and form, but they are clear in one shape.

These markings are of Gods that she knows, from the many stories that she has heard about them. They are the shapes and forms that the gods have presented themselves to human beings on earth. Could it be that these are the actual gods? Cath isn't sure. But what she is sure about is that they are all very beautiful.

These must be the gods, though, she thinks. The way they are having all their needs met by the nymphs around them is all they can be, the only thing that makes sense to her. She watches from behind a bush, hoping that it doesn't change into anything that will expose her. But the whole scene seems to have stabilized now, everything around this clearing having chosen a shape and sticking to it.

Everyone, young and old, there are older looking gods; seems to be in a festive mood. Cath notices their mischievous, carefree nature, as they play and joke, carrying out elaborate tricks on one another. But they mostly play their tricks on one another, though, not any of the nymphs. These women, and some men, seem to know their place, to serve.

She watches this scene for what seems like forever, enjoying the various scenes playing out in front of her. She has to stop herself from giggling out loud, nervous that she will be found out. It's still too soon for them to know that she is here. Eventually, she pries herself away from this spectacle and continues her exploration of the Otherworld.

The gods that she comes across seem very approachable,

but Cath still keeps herself hidden. She almost expects the scene to disappear and she will be back beside the loch, under the trees, with her horse grazing nearby. She had all but forgotten about her horse, and she wonders if it too, perhaps stumbled over into this world. She makes a note to look out for it too.

She continues to observe the Gods, trying to see which one to approach, unsure of how they will respond to having a real human being in their midst. She remembers her home now, for the first time really remembers it, and what is at stake if they are taken down by the armies. She has got to pluck up the courage to ask the gods to help them, and she has to do it soon. She is not sure how long she has been in the Otherworld, not sure how long a day is, and so the sense of urgency builds in her quickly until she is once again very anxious about the survival of her people.

But the gods seem to be more concerned with their festivals than they are with human affairs, not once does she see or hear them talking about what is happening in the real world. She doesn't know if they will be willing to help her, therefore, or if they'll even hear her out. How can she choose a god to present her case to, when they all appear so nonchalant, she wonders?

She comes across another clearing and notices that the atmosphere is more jovial than in the last scene. She chooses a hiding place carefully and watches as this scene too plays out in front of her. For a moment she forgets the real reason that she must have stumbled upon this secret place, the only reason in fact. She reasons that a god, any god, some god, must have heard her call out to them, and so opened up a way for her to enter this world.

Cath watches as the afternoon becomes a festival, filled with play and happiness. She is reminded of the festival to

Belenos that her people have just had, and again she misses home. She thinks of her father and Eogan, two men that she has grown up with and admired, left to fight a war that they did not cause. She must find a way to approach the gods quickly before she loses these two men.

The gods will definitely be able to help them, she thinks. How can they not, after all, with all the gifts and offerings her people have made to them. For as long as she can remember, her people have been holding festivals to gods that few but the Druids and seers have ever seen, believing in the protection and prosperity promised. Well, now the gods had to deliver, and she would tell them as much.

She goes through the Otherworld feeling very exposed suddenly. The gods must know that she is here, or at least the nymphs. And they would have definitely let the gods know of her intrusion. Cath catches the gaze of one of the gods and it is clear to her that the gods have realized that there is a human amongst them!

It's now, or never!!!

CHAPTER 6

THE OTHERWORLD

"COME, COME, MY DEAR..." A female god summons her out of hiding. She searches for the name of this goddess, but it escapes her. She is truly a sight, beautiful from the tip of her head to the soles of her feet. Even her fingers are very attractive so that Cath moves towards them despite herself.

Everyone watches Cath intently as she approaches the gods and takes a seat that seems to have been reserved especially for her. Cath feels their eyes piercing through her, warm and unobtrusive, like the rays of the sun on a spring morning. She looks around, trying to make out each of the gods that she is suddenly surrounded by.

Still, the names of the gods escape her, so she lets it go, albeit temporarily. She sits down, again, despite herself, and watches the spectacle unfold in front of her. The nymphs are dancing now, for the amusement of the gods, and the gods are thoroughly enjoying it.

The dance seems to go on for an eternity. Cath is once again anxious, looking around to see which god she is going to entreat. Maybe she should just entreat all the gods present at this festival, she thinks. Maybe she will stand a better chance of getting at least one of them to listen to her now that she has most of the gods in one place.

But again, she is distracted by the beauty before her, and the beauty around her. She just stares at everything unfolding in front of her; her mouth half-opened, almost salivating. Cath has to bring her hands to her mouth to silence herself from gasping. Eventually, she just lets herself enjoy the experience.

By the time the nymphs have finished their dance Cath is well and truly mesmerized. She has to shake her head to free the images from her mind, but it is impossible. The images play around in her head as vividly as anything that she has ever experienced before.

Cath looks around at the gods who are now also looking at her. They stare at her curiously so that she is suddenly very uncomfortable. She wants to say something, but she thinks that it is too soon; so she just sits back and lets them watch her.

After the longest moment in her life, nobody has spoken to her, and she wonders if she should not perhaps say something. Again, she reasons that it is too soon, and so she just sits still and watches the gods watching her.

The moments seem to fuse into each other now, the silence deathly. Cath suddenly feels like she is a living statue that everyone has come to see, and touch. Some of the nymphs touch her face and her hair. She just lets them, knowing that if they are going to do what she wants, she has to get them very comfortable with her being amongst them.

It feels to her now that everything is lingering, long and languid passages of time that she is not sure are passing at all. Her focus shifts between the nymphs that are touching her, to the gods and goddesses that are looking at her, and to the reason she finds herself in the Otherworld. This is an almost confusing state of mind, but she reminds herself that she needs to stay very focused.

One of the nymphs takes Cath's hand suddenly and she is on her feet. Still surrounded by these ethereal beauties, she is whisked away before she even has a moment to comprehend what is happening. She barely has a moment to wonder where she is being taken to, or why?

Cath once again finds herself in the midst of incredible beauty. She looks around her new world in wonder and amazement, but the thought of her home and what is about to happen there is not too far from her mind. She looks around her at the nymphs, wondering if they might perhaps give her insight into the gods, giving her some clue as to whom she might approach.

But the nymphs seem to be more focused on other more trivial things. They are more worried about Cath's appearance, something that she herself has not paid too much attention to for the past while. Actually, she has never been too concerned about what she looks like. Even when she was to meet Eogan, she would just run a brush through her hair. That was the long and short of her beauty regime.

Surrounded by these beautiful women though, she is suddenly very self-conscious. How could she not be? They are all incredibly beautiful. Their flawlessness slaps her across the face like the leaves of the trees on her face earlier. So much so that she wishes that they would transform her into one of them too, even if it was just for the duration of her time here.

This is exactly what happens. Before she has a moment to object, she is being swiftly transformed into a nymph. Part of her wants to object, part of her does not. She actually starts to thoroughly enjoy this experience, and she almost hates herself for liking it so much, but there is no way out of it, she feels, the nymphs are determined to transform her into one of them.

The transformation is magnificent. They are extremely pleased with themselves as they turn her around, observing their handy work. They make minor adjustments to their work, although they have it perfect already. Still, though, they try to improve on it, and remarkably, they manage to do just that!

The wreath of flowers that crowns her head is spectacular too, as it contains bulbs and beautiful blossoms that are weaved together seemingly effortlessly. The blossoms seem to mesh so that they form a perfect ring, and this ring sits perfectly on her head, with her hair braided in delicate plaits.

Her skin too looks flawless. Her face is milky white with the slightest hint of red on her cheeks. She almost does not recognize herself when she catches her reflection in the nearby pond. Her hands and feet seem to have transformed too, looking very soft and delicate, not at all as if she has just trekked through the wilderness.

She finds this transformation disturbing. It seems to be happening inside of her too, and she tries to shake this awkward feeling from her. Her mind is suddenly filled with images of her mother, a woman she has never seen in the time that she would be old enough to remember her, and yet she is sure that she sees her mother in the woman's eyes staring back at her through the water.

Cath goes to that place inside where she misses her mother, that place where she knows her and has spoken to her of many things, things that a daughter can only speak of to her mother. She hates the part of herself that knows that this is just a dream, and wishes with everything in her for that part of her to be forcibly removed from her.

This is not possible, however. She knows this. She accepts this. Still, though, she hates it. She hates that there is nothing that she can do to see her mother again, at least not in this life. She wonders where her mother might be in this world that she finds herself in. Is she even here? Where do people go when they die, she asks herself? Where do they really go?

Just before she loses herself completely to this question, one of the nymphs touches her face. She looks into the young woman's piercing blue eyes but says nothing. She has no words to say what she is feeling. It has always been like this. She has never been able to find the words that will give voice to how she truly feels about her mother.

The nymphs come closer to her. They all just stare at her, wondering what could possibly be going on in her mind. One of them reaches for her face and catches the tear rolling down her cheek. She wipes it away on her dress as though it is a very bad thing. To Cath, it definitely is.

They take her by the hand and start to show her around the Otherworld. This guided tour distracts her a little from the feelings inside her so that she appreciates it. Without uttering a word, they seem to understand that this is exactly what she needs. Even the anxiety of what is happening back home seems to be a distant thought. It still tugs at her though, however faintly. She just lets herself be dragged along through the Otherworld, marveling at everything that she sees. It could be much worse for her, she tells herself.

They pick berries and fruits, eating them as they go. They sip from the streams and brooks that they pass. Not that Cath is hungry, mind you, but she just has to taste all these beautiful fruits. The nymphs also eat, just for the sake.

They take one or two bites and then pass the fruit on to Cath, who takes it without hesitation.

After a while, Cath starts to feel an urgency tug at her again. She feels as though time is passing, but looking around, she sees no change in the sun's position in the sky. She pulls the closest nymph to her by the hand and asks her if she can talk to her alone. Suddenly everyone is quiet and looking at her so that she feels like she was shouting. She knows, however, that she was just whispering. Obviously, her whispers were very loud. There are clearly no secrets in the Otherworld.

She suddenly feels like everyone is waiting for her to speak. She cannot, however, feel like there are too many ears around. She knows that she has to though before it is too late. Cath looks up at the sun again and finds it strange that the orange orb has not moved at all. For all she knows, days could have gone by.

"Which of them is the nicest?" she asks eventually.

"Them?" Again, it seems like all the nymphs speak at once.

"The gods... which one of them would hear what I have to say... to ask?" She asks this question of all the nymphs around her, knowing now that trying to get one aside will be impossible now anyway.

"Ask them what... dear?" The closest nymph to her now speaks.

"Well, there is this army... back home... and we're surrounded..." she starts, but then they are moving again. The nymphs seem to have short attention spans so that they cannot absorb her full sentences. She starts to stutter, trying to get everything out of her; but it is impossible, and soon enough she is being shown another beautiful creature, not quite a bird, not quite an anything, just beautiful!

Cath tries to get the words out again but fails. Her words seem to be ignored repeatedly so that she eventually just keeps her mouth shut. Instead, she practices in her head what she will say to the gods when she again finds herself before them and moves through the Otherworld with a certain detachment. Her mind is preoccupied suddenly with the matter at hand so that she actually cannot wait to see the gods again.

Around every corner, she hopes beyond hope that she will stumble upon another god, maybe two. She thinks that she will know just what to say to them now, but still, she runs over it repeatedly in her head; and with every turn, she hopes that she can spot even one of the deities that she is now so desperate to see.

"Where are they?" she asks eventually.

"They're everywhere..." Is the answer, emphatic, so that she knows that the gods are probably watching them right now. She looks around her, not expecting to see any of them, but then again, maybe she just might. Cath looks ahead of her again, carefully moving ahead, her mind racing once more with the possibility of bumping into the gods, wanting desperately to despite her apprehension.

The gods are watching, mind you. They have their eyes fixed closely on Cath, listening closely to everything that she is trying to say. The gods manage to piece together the sentences that she is trying to make, and they look at each other. What will they have to say to her when eventually she asks them what is on her mind?

And who is it that brought her here, they wonder. A human does not just stumble on the Otherworld, after all. Again, they look at one another, nobody asking what's on their mind. One thing is clear, though, that they have a few questions for Cath, and for each other. They will probably wait to ask one another what they need to. Cath, on the other hand, will have to answer their questions sooner rather than later.

Finally, Cath and the nymphs come upon a clearing. The meadow is beautiful, with every color of spring. There are the same blossoms that are in her hair all around her suddenly so that she loses her breath momentarily. When she catches it again, the blossoms around her have changed a different color, still as beautiful, but different. She had forgotten how spectacular this place was.

Suddenly, seemingly out of nowhere, the gods start to appear and take their place on the far end of the meadow. They are not all present mind you, but Cath does not mind, just as long as she gets the ear of some of them; and from what she can tell, the main gods are present at this new gathering.

Slowly, slowly, she makes her way to the center of the meadow, and the closer she comes to the gods, the more nervous she gets. Suddenly the whole world seems to be looking at her, and she feels like a little girl about to ask her father for something huge. There is no time for fear now though, and there is nowhere to turn and run. She makes her way to the side of the meadow with the gods, and once she gets before them, she bows down low.

The gods are silent. They watch her closely, enthralled by the change they see in her. She had even forgotten that she has gone through this transformation. She has even forgotten what she looks like now. With no mirror or pond at hand, she has nothing to remind her just how beautiful she now is. She has always been beautiful, but now she looks breathtaking. Her hair falls around her face in the breeze now, so that her eyes are covered. Then the wind blows her hair out of her face, and she looks up at last.

She comes face to face with Dagda, the father of the gods. Their eyes lock, and she feels suddenly as though all her secrets are exposed. Cath looks away because she feels that her soul is suddenly laid bare. It is a strangely liberating experience.

CHAPTER 7

THE GODS in front of her are human, too; or at least they appear to be. She finds this strange, but she almost understands that this is probably for her benefit. Then again, they all have intricate markings on their bodies, their arms, chests, and some on their back that give you a clue as to who they are. So maybe we are not so different from the gods, after all, she thinks.

She looks at each one of them, beautiful and unique. Not the way people are beautiful and unique back on earth mind you, somehow better. She looks at the markings on them so that she knows who they are. One thing is clear though, one of them is clear— Dagda.

But he doesn't speak to her. The father of the gods is silent, just observing her with a hint of curiosity on his face. Cath cannot keep her eyes off him though, even though he is not the one speaking to her.

"What is it that we can do for you my dear?" a goddess asks her, although Cath cannot get to her name right now.

"My people..." she starts, after what must be a long

silence because the gods are all looking at her quizzically now.

"Go on my dear, you are, after all, in front of the council of the gods...Speak freely!" Epona's voice is full of authority and gentle all at the same time. She sounds like a mother and father all at once, so that Cath is not sure if the words are coming out of her mouth at all.

But it is Epona speaking, and Cath hangs on her every word. Another long silence follows before she clears her throat and speaks at last. She has after all been given permission to speak by the mother of the gods.

"My people are surrounded by a combined Greek and Roman army. There is no chance of escape for anyone. The combined force of these armies is 300 000 strong, at least. We are vastly outnumbered. You have to help us!" There are many other things that Cath wants to say to the gods, but she also does not want to get ahead of herself.

The gods look from her to one another. They watch her curiously as she speaks, some of them seem to giggle, almost as if they are wondering at her audacity for asking them to assist them with their current crisis. They look at her with increasing intensity so that Cath is suddenly fearful. This is no time for fear, however, she tells herself. She must be bold.

Oenghus looks at her with particular intrigue and interest. He looks at his father, Dagda, and notices that he too is looking at Cath strangely. He recognizes the look mind you, having seen his father look at a woman that way before. Oenghus does not like that his father is looking at Cath this way, knowing what this means. He cannot imagine going against his father for Cath's affection.

The gods confer among themselves now, so that Cath does not hear what they are saying. She looks closely at them, but it is as if they are speaking with each other using nothing but their minds. She sees their mouths moving, but hears nothing. They, however, seem to understand one another and respond accordingly.

Cath feels like she is trapped in a glass cocoon, able to see everything that is going on around her, but unable to hear anything, or respond in any way. She just has to watch the events unfold in front of her as a spectator, no matter how much she wants to participate in them. It is an incredibly frustrating feeling. She has no choice though, but to let it play out.

She catches Oenghus staring at her, as well as Dagda. They are trying obviously not to look, but they apparently cannot help themselves. Again she feels like she is thoroughly laid bare before these two gods, father, and son, looking through her as if they see her, and yet they do not. It is a strange feeling that she cannot shake.

Eventually, all the gods are looking at her again, none of them speaking. She looks down again, feeling like she should, but as quickly she raises her eyes. She reminds herself that this is no time for her to be coy, and that fear will get her nowhere now. She is already in the Otherworld, and she is before the gods. How this has happened, she does not know. One thing is clear, however, that this is the opportunity of a lifetime.

Dagda speaks finally. His voice fills the space and it sounds like he is speaking all around Cath. There is the feeling that she is dreaming again, and Cath does not even try to rid herself of this feeling anymore. She just accepts it and decides to deal with it. Her focus is on the words falling from Dagda's mouth though; she really has to strain to make them out.

Not that his words are inaudible mind you, it is just that

they sound like they are falling into each other, like leaves in a bag. She catches the beginning of some words, and the end of others so that the two combine to form strange new words that she has never heard before. As she listens to his voice, however, its tone rich and warm, the words start to fall on her ears in the order that he is saying them.

"Your words are sincere, and you have been heard, my dear. You will need to give us a moment to think about everything that you are asking us, I'm sure you understand?" Dagda speaks so clearly that Cath cannot even remember that just moments earlier she could not make out what he was saying.

"A moment... how long is..." Cath begins, but she stops speaking as Epona and Dagda both raise their hands. She looks away briefly, catches herself, and then looks Dagda square in his face again so that he knows that he can continue speaking and that he has her full attention once more.

"A moment my dear is as long as it needs to be. You will spend your time with the nymphs while we deliberate. I'm sure that they can keep you sufficiently distracted while we talk." Dagda says this as a final word so that Cath knows that any protest will be useless. She looks around her at the nymphs who are smiling with glee, excited by their new charge.

As she walks away from the gods, she looks back at them and sees them once again locked in conversation that she cannot hear. She catches Oenghus's eyes fixed on her. He does not look away from her at all, and she holds his gaze. There is no way that she can escape his look, and she is not sure if she wants to.

The nymphs pull her away excitedly. They fix her hair and her face, adjust her floral ring on her head, and check her dress. Once they are sure that she is perfect again, they admire their handiwork. The nymphs seem unable to control their giggles so that Cath cannot help herself but to admire their almost childish wistfulness.

Cath is chaperoned by nymphs around the Otherworld. They show her this wonder and that wonder, slowly though, because it is obvious that it is all a bit too much for Cath. What she has already seen does not even compare to what she now sees, so that she really has to take moments to catch her breath.

The nymphs continue to fiddle with Cath, determined to turn the warrior princess into a nymph. They are succeeding too, and as she moves with them through the Otherworld, she does not even notice that the transformation is happening. It would overwhelm her if it were not such a wonderful experience. She almost forgets the reason that she is here.

Cath moves through the Otherworld looking more and more beautiful as she goes. Many of the gods watch this transformation happening right before their eyes. They notice her features softening even more, and this intrigues them. How can someone so beautiful become even more so, they wonder?

The changes in Cath are both subtle and obvious so that they confuse even the gods. The nymphs have really done a fantastic job on Cath so that she is more appealing and beautiful than even the most beautiful amongst them. This was their goal, their intention. They know that this will please one god in particular; and perhaps a few more other ones as well.

Dagda has been watching this closely, with growing interest. He is not the one who summoned Cath to the Otherworld, never involving himself on this level with human affairs. Now that she is here, however, he plans to make the most of this situation. He wants her, and as the father of the gods, he knows he can have her. He just needs to approach this very carefully.

Humans are not like the gods at all. The gods are passionate and carefree, taking what they want and whom they want at will. Humans have a problem with feelings. They need to feel everything before they make the simplest choices. This is a very complex characteristic; one that Dagda is sure he can manipulate.

Cath notices this interest. She watches Dagda watching her, albeit from a distance. She wonders why he does not approach her and tells her what the gods have decided. It is starting to feel like they are toying with her as if the gods are just playing one of their elaborate games with her.

It does not help that she has lost her concept of time. She really has no idea how much time has passed since she arrived in the Otherworld. She has no idea, but it feels like it should be days, with all the transformation that she has undergone. But the sun still hangs high in the sky, in the same place it was when she arrived. She tries not to think about this.

She watches with interest how Dagda looks at her from a distance, and she wonders why he doesn't come up to her and say what is on his mind. He is after all the father of the gods, and he can say whatever he feels he wants to say, she thinks. Little does she know that this is all part of a very crafty, very clever, very well thought out strategy!

So she just accepts the gazes, without thinking too much about it, and wondering when he will let her know what they have decided. This is starting to get a little frustrating for her, so much so that she is starting to feel a little distracted, her head filling once again with thoughts of home.

Cath has not realized it yet, but Dagda is not just attracted to her physically. He has fallen in love with her, the passion she displayed at the meeting before the council, and the transformation she has undergone since, how it has not removed any of the fire from her eyes. He is truly smitten. There is nobody that has moved him this way in all the Otherworld, and he knows that he must have her.

Finally, he comes out of the shadows and into the glorious light that soaks the Otherworld. He comes up to Cath and pierces her with his eyes again. Cath tries not to look at him in his face, but she cannot help herself. He loves the fact that she is not too intimidated by him so as to look away. She challenges him in ways that he has never been challenged before, and this intrigues him more than anything that he has ever intrigued him before.

"How are you finding the Otherworld Cath?" he asks her. She cannot deny that she loves the way her name sounds as it falls from his lips. It is actually just that she has not heard her name in the longest while, and it sounds surreal.

"How long before you are clear on my request... I'm not sure how much time I have to..." Cath starts, but she stops speaking when she sees that Dagda is not listening to her. He clearly has something else on his mind.

"I want to get to know you a little better..." Dagda is clear about what he wants. He is sure of himself and this confidence translates effortlessly into the way he speaks. But Cath is frustrated again by his avoidance of the real reason that she is here.

"I am promised to another!" Cath says the words, even before she can think of the consequences of saying them.

She immediately wishes that she could take back the words that she spoke so honestly. It is too late, however.

"And you are in love with this man?" Dagda asks her, this so matter-of-factly that Cath feels she must just be honest with him. There is no turning back now that the words have come out of her mouth.

"I am, very much so, yes," she responds. She cannot think that there is another way to approach this situation, so unexpected.

"I would never force you into anything that you do not want. I just hope that you can give me the opportunity to..." Dagda is the one who does not finish his sentence now, Cath putting her finger to his lips to silence him. She finds his lips warm and cool at the same time so that her finger lingers there for a moment too long. She removes it quickly and she would put it in her pocket if she had any.

This situation has really taken a turn, and not a good one. Cath is nervous and she has no idea what to say to him anymore. Dagda too is quiet now, just looking at her, looking through her. They stare at one another for a moment longer before Dagda pulls himself from Cath and disappears into the nearby grove.

Another god is smitten with Cath, however. Oenghus has observed the changes in Cath, too, so that he makes up his mind to woo her. Actually, he fell in love with her from the moment he first laid eyes on her. And this was not even in the Otherworld.

He first laid eyes on her on a visit to the real world, when he saw her at the festival of Beltaine, a few years before. He has sneaked onto the real plane often since then, just to see her. Even when she was practicing on her own for the battle ahead, he was there, watching from the shadows.

When she left her home for Scotland, Oenghus was there too. He watched over her on her journey, just to make sure that she was safe. And when the opportunity presented itself, he opened up the door for her to find herself crossing over into the Otherworld. When she crossed over, however, Oenghus could not believe it, and so he kept it to himself. For now, nobody needs to know that he is the reason that Cath has ended up here.

"Father, can I speak with you?" Oenghus approaches his father cautiously.

"Yes, yes, son, what is it?" Dagda really loves his son.

"I think I'm in love with her father!" He gets right into it, not feeling awkward about discussing this with his father suddenly. All caution is gone now, and he feels free to have the conversation that he needs to have with his father.

"The human?" Dagda asks, although he already knows the answer.

"Yes, father!"

"And what do you intend doing about the way that you feel?" Dagda is curious to the response that his son will give him to this question. He looks intently at him, waiting for the words to come out of his mouth. He hopes to get some idea of what he might do to win Cath over.

"I don't know father, but I intend to show her the life that she can have if she stays here with us... with me!" Oenghus really does not know what to do; or what else to say.

"And what if she is already in love with someone else?" Dagda needs to know how much his son really knows about Cath.

"I know she is... but if we don't help them with the war, he won't be a problem anymore." Oenghus is suddenly clear, knowing what he needs to do to keep Cath here.

"And if we don't help them, what do you think that will do to her?" Dagda presses.

"It will hurt her, for a while, but she will soon accept that there is nothing for her to go back for, and I will be free to love her, to have her." Oenghus is a lot like his father was in his youth. Dagda looks at his son and he is astonished by how much of himself he sees in the young god.

"Well, it has not yet been decided if we will get involved or not. While we make up our minds, she will be treated like a goddess of the Otherworld. Maybe, just maybe, this will persuade her to stay." Dagda suddenly has a plan to keep Cath here, to encourage her to stay. He looks away from his son, not wanting him to see this plan that is forming in his head

After a brief meeting with the nymphs, they know what to do. Cath is treated more and more like a goddess, something that she does not understand. She does not even like it. But what else can she do, while she waits for the gods to make up her mind? She just has to accept everything that is happening to her.

She looks around for her horse and wonders what could have happened to her weapons. This thought almost consumes her, even though she is not given the time to entertain even her own thoughts. There is something about being treated differently from everyone else that has always made her uncomfortable. But she assumes that this is just the way of the gods.

Cath has no idea how she can get back to the real world anyway so that she knows that she has to keep the gods happy. There is really very little that she can do about the way she is being treated, except to pretend to enjoy it. It is a very uncomfortable situation for her though.

Dagda is well and truly smitten with her. So is his son

Oenghus. This could be very complicated for Cath, but it is not until she is aware of this complication that she realizes how much of a challenge this situation could present. She has no idea how her life is about to change; and not in a good way at all.

CHAPTER 8

OENGHUS FINALLY GETS CATH ALONE. She is near a lake with her chaperones, who are catering to her every need. Just as she is about to ask one of them about the sun that never seems to set, Oenghus comes out of the shade of the grove, and all the nymphs scatter.

Cath has no idea why they all leave, but it becomes clear soon enough. Oenghus comes in close to her and takes her face in his hands. His grip is firm so that she cannot look away. She succumbs to him so that she is almost malleable in his hands.

He likes this. Oenghus did not expect that he would have this effect on her, but he is very happy that he does. He has seen Cath with Eogan, and he has seen how she has been with him. He thinks he sees this same look in her eyes now.

But it is not love that he sees in her eyes. Cath is just tired of all this wooing that is going on around her. And this exhaustion softens her face even more so that she appears to be drunk in love. She is not. The look in her eyes is not to be mistaken for passion either; she just has a natural fire in them that she cannot hide.

"I think I'm in love with you," he says to her eventually. She cannot say that she is surprised by this revelation, thinking of the encounter she had with Dagda earlier.

"I am promised to another," she responds, hoping that this will be enough for him to stop going in the direction that she sees this conversation going in.

"I know," he responds. It is unexpected that she looks at him with a question mark in her eyes.

"You know?" Cath asks him.

"I know," Oenghus confirms. Cath doesn't need to ask him any further, knowing that he probably does know. There are really more things on earth than she can understand, not that she even wants to anyway.

"So, what is the thinking about my request?" she asks, to move the conversation away from anything that has to do with love.

"They are still thinking about it!" Oenghus replies to her nonchalantly.

"How long do you think they will be thinking about it?" Cath really needs to know.

"You will know once they've decided!" Oenghus answers her with a tone that lets her know that she will not get any more out of him. She makes a note to seek out Dagda on the matter.

The opportunity comes sooner than she expects. The nymphs prepare Cath for a private dinner invitation from Dagda. This is a most necessary meeting, one that Cath knows she needs to have. This does not take the edge off mind you, and she has to will herself to relax.

She is taken by her chaperones to a grove that she has never been to before. Upon arrival, she is ushered beneath a canapé, a beautiful setup that would be made more beautiful if she were meeting Eogan underneath it. But she is not. She is meeting the father of the gods, a man who has declared his love for her already. This makes her very nervous.

"Hello, my dear. Good evening!" Dagda sounds like he does not believe himself when he says 'good evening', looking around at the sun-soaked Otherworld.

"Is it?" Cath asks, seeing the look that Dagda throws around him.

"Well no, not exactly. But you must be hungry?" Dagda senses that he needs to be honest with Cath, who is clearly very clever.

"You don't need to worry about your people. We have that under control. Now, can you relax and eat?" It sounds unnatural when he asks her to eat, particularly because she knows that he is probably not going to eat. The gods never eat. They never seem to eat. Which is understandable sort of, she thinks.

To her surprise, Dagda helps himself to some of the fruit in front of them. It looks natural and not at all strange. She eats despite herself, and the fruit before her meets her every expectation. It does not even feel like the only thing that they are eating is fruit. Each bite tells her pallet and her tongue a million stories that she does not want to know the ending to.

Dagda promises that all will be well and that they will help the Celts with the upcoming war. He reminds her that he is the father of the gods and that the others will do what he says. He speaks with clarity that sets Cath's mind at ease. She cannot help thinking that they are wasting time, however, and she wonders what she can do to speed this up even more.

Dagda will not discuss this any further, however. He proceeds with the dinner in front of him, although it feels more like a lunch to Cath. She nibbles on pieces of fruit now, her mind racing, both with the wonderment of the flavors, as well as the thoughts creeping over her, as to how she can get the gods to take action quicker.

Cath is confused when Dagda finally leaves her to her thoughts. The nymphs are around her once more, and they look at her with questions in their eyes, questions that they cannot yet articulate. Never before have they had to deal with emotion. It is a very new experience for the naïve nymphs.

One thing is clear, however. Dagda is in love with Cath. She is not even sure whether it is real love or just lust, what with the playful nature of the gods. But she is certain that he wants her, and this is a complication that she cannot deal with. Cath now realizes that she is caught in a dangerous game, one that she never anticipated that she would ever have to play in her lifetime.

Cath wishes that she could sleep, but she cannot. She does not need to and this is both a blessing and a curse. It is a curse, because if she was just able to sleep, then maybe she could wake from this nightmare. It is a blessing because she has learned from the nymphs that the gods have called another meeting. She needs to be there.

The nymphs, however, tell her that she has been expressly forbidden from attending. The gods will discuss her situation and then they will inform her of the outcome. She is to stay away from the meeting until the gods call her to let her know what they have decided. This is how it will be.

Cath cannot accept this, though. She is determined to hear what the gods discuss. There is no way that she cannot be there. The nymphs understand this. They get where she is coming from and they agree to help her. They will show her where the gods have gathered, but Cath has to remain unseen. She needs to stay out of sight, so as not to incur the wrath of the gods.

She gets just close enough to hear what the gods are saying, but she remains out of view. She cannot help but think that the gods know that she is there, lurking in the shadows. If they do know of her presence, though, they say nothing.

"We will help them!" Dagda speaks first this time.

"But we never get involved in human affairs!" Epona objects.

"Except at their festivals where we are offered gifts and praise," Dagda counters.

"Still, we are the gods. They must serve us, and praise us!" Epona is determined to make a point that Cath does not really like, but she has to restrain herself from making herself visible so that the gods do not stop talking.

"We are the gods, and we have a duty to protect our people." Dagda is insistent.

"They have never needed our protection before, always managing to get themselves out of the messes they find themselves in. And they have always praised us for these successes that we really had nothing to do with. Why should this time be any different?" Epona skates freely on the thin ice that is Cath's heart. Cath finds herself more and more disappointed with the gods, never having realized before just how selfish these deities are.

"Have you not heard a word that the young woman has said? They are completely overwhelmed. There is no hope of success this time. We must help them. We will help them!" Dagda and Epona speak to each other now; the other gods are present just watching the exchange that is happening in front of them. "They will think that we have abandoned them. We cannot have that!"

The debate rages for hours and Cath becomes anxious. The nymphs hold on to her arm to prevent her from barging in on the meeting. She half fights them, and half doesn't. She ends up wanting to just disappear and be back at home so that she can help her father and Eogan. She just wants to hold Eogan and have the whole world melt away.

But she can't, so she just listens to the gods as they go back and forth with their arguments. Sometimes it seems that Dagda is going to pull rank and just order the gods to help the Celts. At other times, it seems like Dagda does not have the final say, and he has to get the buy-in of all the gods, otherwise, this will just have been a waste of Cath's time.

"After we have helped them, she will not be able to leave here," Epona says, as a matter of fact. Dagda has been waiting for one of the gods to say these words. He cannot have them see his own enthusiasm for her staying, especially not Oenghus, who has told him already that he is in love with the human.

"So you are in agreement, then, that we must help them?" Dagda just needs confirmation of what he is hearing.

"The question is, will she be in agreement about staying here after we have helped them!" Epona asks this question as though she already knows the answer.

"She will have little choice in the matter!" Dagda sounds sure of himself.

Cath is still listening to the gods, the nymphs around her excited by the possibility of this addition. Cath is taken aback, not believing what she hears.

The gods continue to conspire about this new situation that they find themselves in. They suddenly seem very intent on keeping Cath as one of their own, something that Dagda does not object to. Neither does Oenghus. He has to hide his excitement at this unexpected turn of events.

Cath has heard enough. She pulls away from the nymphs and walks away from where the gods are gathered. She needs to think about everything that she has heard and process it all. Things really have escalated rather quickly in this place where time seems to standstill.

She finds herself alone in a grove, the nymphs giving her the space she needs to think. All the words spoken by Dagda and Epona come at her from every direction, so that she has to block her ears in an attempt to silence them. She cannot though— try as she might, she remembers every syllable.

Can the gods really force her to stay here in the Otherworld, she asks herself. Surely they cannot, surely they cannot keep her here against her will. There must be some mistake. She cannot believe the words that she is sure that she has heard. This is just suddenly very wrong to her, and she feels like she is being held to ransom so that her people can get the help that they so desperately need.

But it is a ransom that she will gladly make, she reminds herself. She tells herself that if the gods help them to win this battle, then she will stay behind and never see her people again. The thought that she will never see her family again suddenly settles over her and she breaks down at last.

She weeps bitterly so that the nymphs are taken aback by this. They escape into the safety of the trees and just watch her through the leaves. There is something that moves inside each one of them so that they want to hold her, but they have no response to Cath's display of emotion.

There is an odd silence that settles over the grove now so that the only sound that is audible is the sound of Cath's weeping.

Eventually, she gathers herself sufficiently to completely process what is going on. She accepts how things have turned out, and she accepts that she will probably have to stay back in the Otherworld after they have helped the Celts win the war. She only has to do this one thing, and that will ensure the safety of her people from the Greek and Roman armies that have gathered to destroy them.

She resolves to play along, to go with what the gods expect of her. She cannot see herself with Dagda, or Oenghus, so that thought does not even cross her mind. She does, however, have to ensure that a strong army fights with her people, and so she must do what she must do to make sure of this.

Eventually, the nymphs come out of the trees, and they surround Cath, who is pulling herself together. They go about making her beautiful again and drying her tears. They replace the floral ring on her head, and they put a few more braids in her hair. Cath is suddenly reminded of all the stories she heard about her mother, about how she would have her hair brushed and braided by her hand-maiden. A deep sadness fills her again.

Looking even more beautiful than before, Cath is invited to a picnic. She has no idea who it is that has sent her the invitation, but it does not matter to her. One thing is clear, she is about to be told about the gods' decision. She will have to dig deep within herself to find the strength to agree to the terms of them helping the Celts.

She almost understands where the gods are coming from. They cannot risk her returning to the real world, where she will reveal the secret mysteries of the Other-world. Cath makes up her mind not to argue with them on this. She just has to make sure that the gods get to her people on time.

Cath arrives at the wonderful picnic setup, with all the details that she would have expected from Eogan. More so in fact, with elements that can only be expected from a god. There are multi-colored flying creatures around the canapé that has been set up. At a closer glance, these creatures look like cats. This is mesmerizing so that Cath does not see the god waiting for her at first.

Then she catches Oenghus. He is looking away from her, but as soon as she comes out into the open, he turns around and looks at her. Their eyes lock, but instantly Cath wishes that it was Dagda seated underneath the silk covering. She wishes that Dagda had called her so that he could give her some clarity on the way forward. What good can come out of this meeting with Oenghus?

"Hello, Cath!" Oenghus sounds nothing like his father, and Cath notices for the first time. Maybe it is that he is trying so hard to be gentle, to come across as warm and inviting. She does not know. She cannot possibly know.

"Hello..." Cath responds. She cannot search for any further words to say to him, and so all he gets is a hello. But there is not even a moment for her to process what to say next, because Oenghus speaks immediately again.

"Welcome... welcome. How are you? How is every-thing? Are you being treated well?" Too many questions come at her all at the same time so that she does not know which one of them to answer first.

"I'm sorry..." Oenghus apologizes, realizing that he is inundating Cath with questions, probably because of his excitement. She tries to process this apology from a god, which takes her by surprise, especially since she knows how they really are.

"Have the gods made a decision about my request?" Cath asks him immediately what is on her mind. There is a clearly visible line that Cath is not prepared to cross with Oenghus or with his father and she is determined to stay on her side of the line. She hopes that her question goes to show him this point.

"There has been a decision made, and the council will call you soon to let you know what that is. That is not a choice that I am free to discuss with you. There is something though, that I would like to discuss with you at this time." Oenghus makes it clear to Cath that he would like to discuss matters other than what she has asked.

Cath listens to Oenghus's proclamations of love, and he is determined to get her to come around to what he is saying. Cath, however, is not accepting what he is saying. The words are just going over her like water. She does not absorb even one. This picnic seems to be taking very long indeed.

At the end of the picnic, Cath walks away from her suitor, and she is troubled. She wonders how much of this wooing will take place once she is in the Otherworld permanently. The nymphs try to distract her from her thoughts, but it does not last very long, and they are not very successful. Dagda summoned Cath to a dinner meeting shortly after.

This meeting is in secret, and no other god is aware of this. It is in Dagda's own secret grove, and the nymphs are quick to let Cath know that this means that nobody in the Otherworld will even know of this dinner, or what is said at it. This makes Cath very nervous.

"We will help you!" Dagda gets straight to the point.

"Thank you!" Cath knows better than to let him know that she is aware of the meeting that the gods had earlier, or what was said there.

"There is just one condition, however..." He speaks slowly so that his words settle on her and he is sure that she hears everything that he is saying.

"Yes?" Cath asks, although she already knows what the answer is.

"You will have to remain back here in the Otherworld after we have helped you win." Again Dagda waits for her to receive this information, and to give her a chance to respond to what he has just said.

"So I will never see my family again then?" Cath asks, just for clarity.

"No, you won't. But you will live in the bliss of the Otherworld eternally." He says this as though it is a wonderful gift that he is giving to her.

She finds herself missing Eogan even more now, in this moment that she is being told that she will never see him again. She has to find a way to see him, just once. She has to find a way to see her father just one more time before she is committed to staying in this place of strangeness and wonder. It is beautiful, no doubt, but it is not what she wanted for her life.

Dagda proceeds with his own proclamations of love. These are words that she really does not want to hear right now. It is something that she cannot even comprehend at this time. Still, she lets the older god speak, even though she is not really listening to a word that he is saying to her.

"I have really come to care for you, in the time that you have been here. I cannot help myself. It is just how I feel. What do you feel?" Dagda asks her this as though she is just expected to forget everything that is going on in the real world and be suddenly in love with him.

"I can't even think about how I feel right now, I'm afraid!" Cath excuses herself, needing to create distance between herself and this mad situation where she is wanted by two gods, while back on earth, her true love, Eogan, has no idea that she is even alive.

She feels the pressure though, really feels it. She does not know how sincere the gods are about helping her people or even if this help is offered conditionally. They have said that she has to remain here in the Otherworld, and she accepts this. But will she have to choose between these two gods before they go ahead and help her people?

Cath curls up on the soft earth, the sun on her face, and she thinks of these questions while she tries to make sense of the next step that she has to take.

CHAPTER 9

CATH'S PROBLEMS do not stop there. Oenghus realizes what his father is up to. This is very disturbing for him. He had, after all, trusted his father with his own feelings for Cath. But the nymphs are more loyal to the younger god, and so they do not waste any time telling Oenghus what Dagda is up to once they realize this.

"What are you playing at, father?" Oenghus asks his father when he gets him alone.

"What do you mean boy?" Dagda makes their different stations quite clear to the young god so that he does not overstep his mark.

"With Cath." Oenghus is clear about what he is asking his father.

"I'm not playing at anything. There is nothing wrong with a little competition. Surely you will not let this stand in your way?" Dagda's arrogance is almost tangible.

"But father, you are the leader of the gods. There is no competition there. You will have whatever you want; take whatever you want. So what competition is there for her affections? You will obviously win!" Oenghus is obviously pained by this unexpected challenge for Cath.

"The best god will win in the end, boy!" Dagda has a way of ending conversations without expressly saying so.

Oenghus walks away from his father before he says something that he cannot take back. Confused, he needs time alone, time to think about how best he is going to approach this challenge. The best god will win, his father says. His father is the older god; he has been around for a longer time, so he is obviously the best god. Or is he?

Alone, he thinks about this new development. He wonders at what point his father decided that he too wanted Cath. Surely he does not love her. He cannot. It just is not possible. He must just want her for the sake of, the same way he has wanted every nymph that Oenghus has taken a liking to in the past. He has always been out to prove that he is still the superior.

This is something that Oenghus has never understood. He has always been in his father's shadow for as long as he can remember. He is tired of it. There has never been anything that he can do about it. Or at least there has not been until now. Now he has a tangible challenge set before him, one that his father cannot use his influence as the senior god to win.

Cath is a human, and as such, the laws of the Otherworld do not govern her. She will not let herself be told what to do, Oenghus realizes. He knows that she will not. There are a few things that he has learned about Cath from observing her in the real world, and he plans to use these observations to his advantage.

He has learned that she is fiercely independent and that she isn't governed by any man. While she loves Eogan, something that Oenghus has to admit to himself, Eogan does not own her. She dances to the beat of her own drum, and that is part of the attraction for him.

These are things that Dagda doesn't know. He is so accustomed to getting his own way, and when he does not, he demands the things that he wants. This approach will not work with Cath. Oenghus knows this. Dagda does not. This immediately stands the younger god in a much better position for winning Cath's affection.

Still, he does not understand Dagda's behavior. His father has a remarkably childish approach to life, believing that he is entitled to anything that he wants. There is a similarity in their behavior, however, that Oenghus does not want to face. It is easier for him to accept that they are as different as night and day.

In the moments that pass, for they are moments and not days, Cath is caught between father and son. She wants neither of them, but she feels that she must entertain this attention because the gods have not made a move as yet to help the Celts. She is starting to feel that she will have to make a choice between the two, however, if her people are to have any hope.

But none of them have said anything of the sorts. So she isn't even sure if this is a condition for them to help her. She cannot take the risk, though, and so she attends picnics and dinners in the hope that soon they will make a move.

Then something strange happens. Oenghus is summoned by Dagda to his secret grove. He is concerned about what his father might have to say to him. Nevertheless, he is in the grove now, and after taking a moment to compose himself, he crosses over in between the trees, disappearing in effect from the rest of the Otherworld.

Dagda is more like a father to him now, and this surprises Oenghus. He cannot hide his surprise either.

There is something different about his father; something that makes the younger god more than a little uncomfortable.

"I think that I may have been a little presumptuous in my dealings with you earlier my son, and for this, I apologize." Dagda sounds sincere, so much so that Oenghus is even more confused.

"You apologize?" Oenghus wonders what game his father is playing.

"Yes, I am sorry!" Dagda cannot even look at his son now.

"What are you saying, father?" Oenghus needs to be sure of what he is hearing.

"I am saying that perhaps I should not have challenged you for the affections of the human."

"And what exactly does that mean for me now father?" Oenghus needs to understand what his father is actually saying.

"I am saying that you can pursue her and that I will not interfere," Dagda says the words that his son wants to hear.

Cath in the meantime, wonders at the fate of her people. She has no idea what fate has in store for her at all. However, her concern for her people overrides her concern, even for herself. She cannot be concerned about how she is going to end up.

The nymphs, however, are quick to give her the pros and cons of both men. They let her know that Dagda is the father of the gods, and her position among the gods will be solidified if she chooses him. Oenghus, on the other hand, is a younger god, who will treat Cath with more tenderness and care, having spent time in the real world and understanding how humans treat each other.

Cath listens to them, noting both arguments. She

cannot be bothered by these words that are being thrown at her anyway though, her thoughts with Eogan. She cannot accept that she will never see him again, but this is a sacrifice that she needs to make. What is she going to do to make sure that she sees him just one more time at least?

She thinks of her family, too, and of her people. How can she get the gods to stop focusing on wooing her, and concentrate their energies on helping her people? There must be a way around this situation she thinks, but she cannot at the moment think how. This, more than anything else, troubles her.

It hits her suddenly, how she can make everybody, including herself happy. She will speak to the gods and negotiate that she will return with them if they let her fight with her people. This is the only way that she can think of that will give her the opportunity to see Eogan and her father again. She must convince them that this is the only way.

She resolves to be as miserable as possible, which will not be difficult, in the Otherworld, if she does not see her family one more time. She does not even need to speak to them. Even if she sees them across the battlefield, this will be enough for her. She just needs to go across again to the real world one last time, before she can commit to coming back to the Otherworld.

Cath thinks about everything that has happened in such a seemingly short time. She cannot believe that she is now the love interest of two gods. Just a short time ago she was betrothed, planning the life that she would have with Eogan. Her father had accepted him as the man in her life, the one that she would spend the rest of her life with. Now she is here in the Otherworld, and she is being tossed about like a traded jewel that will be sold to the highest bidder.

All she wanted was to get back to her people on time, to help them fight the battle that they were obviously going to lose. She had thought that she would go in the direction of Scotland, not actually pass through, and return in time to fall with her people. It has not turned out that way.

Instead, she crossed over to the Otherworld. How she does not know yet. She is here, though, and she finds herself between two gods, father, and son, who both profess to love her. How can they love her, however, when they do not even know her? They do not know her the way Eogan knows her. They do not know what she likes, or the things that make her sad. They have no idea what motivates her and what moves her to do the things that she has done, the things that she wants to do.

All these things weigh heavily on her mind. There is nothing that she can do to undo what has happened, though, but she can definitely try to get the opportunity to see her family again. The only thing that she can do is to talk to the gods about letting her go back with them when they go to fight the Greeks and the Romans. She knows that she will have to promise that she will come back with them, however, but that is just a sacrifice that she will have to make. There is no other way.

Another thought weighs heavily on her mind. She wonders which of the two gods she will have to marry after this is all over. It is obvious that this is what they want, and it is obvious that she will have to make a choice. But what choice will she make? How will she choose in such a way so as not to jeopardize her people in the future? How will she choose in such a way so as not to jeopardize her people now?

She has heard what the nymphs have said about both gods, but this has not done anything to convince her either way. They have done very little in the way of convincing her which of the gods is a better option. There is no way that they can, she feels. There is nothing that they can say to her to convince her that choosing any one of the two gods would be better for her, not in the least.

Cath lets these thoughts wander around in her head without trying to give them any sort of direction. There is no point in trying to make sense of this situation anymore. She just has to accept the way that things have turned out, and she needs to convince the gods that they must let her go back with them, for one last time.

"I have one condition," she starts, when she once again finds herself before the council of the gods.

"Condition?" Epona asks, almost laughing it off.

"I want to go back with you, to fight with you when you go and save my people." Cath is clear about her statement. It is not a request.

"Impossible!" Cath isn't sure who is saying this, but it seems to reverberate amongst all the gods so that it seems like they are all saying it.

"It is the very least you can allow. You will be ripping me from my home, from everything that I know. The least you can do is allow me to go back with you, to fight along-side my people, to breathe in the air of the Welsh Plains one last time." Cath makes a very impassioned plea.

The gods look to each other, and to Dagda. Surely he will say the words that will stop this nonsense and stop Cath from making ridiculous demands. He does not, however. After looking at the other gods for the longest time he turns his attention to Cath. At last, he speaks. "We will allow it my dear, but you will have to train with our soldiers in preparation for the battle!"

Soldiers? Cath had not even known that the gods had

soldiers. Did they not fight their own battles? Obviously not. This realization is a shock to her, but it is one that she quickly gets over. She is just glad that her request has been met.

She wonders at the training, however. How long will it be? And what will it entail? She needs them to see the urgency of this situation so that they stop all the delays. The gods, however, seem very relaxed so that Cath has to ask, "When will we leave?"

"Soon my dear, very soon. Go now, and rest. Your training will begin shortly." Dagda dismisses her and turns to the other gods to finalize the details of the army that they will send with her to fight the threat.

She is taken by her nymphs to another grove, where they transform her from goddess back to a warrior princess. She is much more comfortable now, and she cannot wait to train and join her people on the field of battle. Her weapons are handed to her. She does not even ask where they have been. She does wonder about her horse, however, but still, she does not ask any of the nymphs where it could be.

Dagda calls Oenghus to him again. He reassures him that he will not interfere with his wooing of Cath any further. He really has done a complete turnabout seemingly, and this is still very uncomfortable for the young god. The situation brings about a complex element to this already fragile relationship, but Dagda seems to be determined to repair this relationship. Oenghus does a very good job of hiding his confusion.

"Thank you father," he manages.

"Now, we must go and prepare for this battle, and bring back the young woman safely so that you can continue to convince her that you can make her happy." Dagda sounds like he means everything that he is saying. Oenghus has no reason not to believe him.

"Yes, father ." That is all Oenghus can say, still mulling the information in his head. What brought about his father's sudden turn in behavior? What could have brought about this change that he sees in his father? He cannot even question it anymore. There is no time for him to question this anymore anyway!

There is a calm that settles over the Otherworld now, in light of the new development. Dagda still wants Cath, but Oenghus must come first. At least now he knows that he will have given his son the chance at happiness, a chance that he has enjoyed many times before. So it is only fair that he affords his son the same opportunity.

The soldiers are excited by the possibility of war. They cannot hide this excitement from each other. There is a new verve in the camps of the gods, and this is very tangible. They are very motivated by the idea that they will spill human blood. They do not even need a reason; they just want the opportunity to get to use their weapons, something that they very seldom get to do.

They start to practice almost immediately. Cath is very excited too by this, that she will see her father again, and Eogan. She practices with a renewed energy, forgetting even the price that she will have to pay for this opportunity. Nothing can dampen her renewed spirit. The new motivation fills her up with hope and promises that her people will be safe, that her father will be safe, and that Eogan will be safe.

She is sure that he will find love again! She has got to believe in his future happiness, even though it will not be with her. He will go on, he must. She tells herself all the things that she does not want to hear but she has to. There is no other way. She throws herself into practicing for the upcoming war and preparing to see her family again.

They all have renewed energy that brings the excitement of the upcoming war across the very fabric of the Otherworld. There is nothing that can get anyone to think of anything else, not anymore. It is really an exciting time.

CHAPTER 10

EOGAN'S THOUGHTS are consumed with Cath. He worries about her safety, and wonders where she is. He wonders what she might be doing right now, or whom she is with. These thoughts are uppermost in his mind. He tries as best as he can to focus on the coming battle. But he also cannot help the thoughts that fill his head.

He tries to keep his mind on the battle. He throws himself deeper and deeper into the preparation. The intensity is visible on his face, and he fights fiercely. There is a determination that underlies his efforts now as if he knows that he will see Cath again if they win this war.

Ailill too spurs him on to train. He keeps him motivated, and he understands what exactly is at stake. There is nothing that they can do about Cath's safety anymore, anyway. And at least they know that she is safe. So at the very least, they do not have that to worry about.

Without Cath here, however, they both have a definite sadness that they cannot hide. How can they, when their only reason for existing is no longer there? They both think of what would have happened to her in enemy hands. This consoles them somewhat, that Cath is away from this mess.

They proceed aggressively with preparations for this battle. Moving the length and breadth of the land, they conscribed every single able-bodied man to join their army. With a formidable force gathered, they still do not come anything close to the combined Greek and Roman army that has surrounded them. But still, they prepare with everything that they have inside of them.

Men are fitted with bronze body armor, covering their chests, and helmets on their heads. They work tirelessly day and night to ensure that the armor fits just perfectly! They are committed to fighting valiantly, and they are determined to give the armies that have come to attack them quite a fight. There really is no other way.

They are provided with shields and slashing swords as well. The blacksmiths really are putting in the time, sweating in the heat of their workrooms, ensuring that they have built considerable artillery. Soon enough the men in the settlement are all armed, and armored. They can focus now on practicing for the war, and getting comfortable with the swords in their hands and the metal skins over their bodies.

The Otherworld has taken on a new feeling too. It has become a military camp, one that closely resembles the camps back home, so that Cath feels almost that she is back home. Cath starts to practice with the gods. She trains with the gods' soldiers in preparation for the battle. This is strange to Cath until somebody explains it to her.

"The thing is," one of the soldiers says, "once in the earth's realm, the gods' power is halved, making them more human. That is why we need to prepare for this fight so that we stand a better chance of winning!"

"But you're the gods... you're the gods. I don't under-stand..." Cath says. She is slightly confused, but she is sure that it will become clear. It is becoming clearer to her, but she cannot help the slight sense of confusion that she feels.

They continue to prepare physically for the war. But the gods do not practice with them, just the gods' warriors. Cath had not even known that the gods had soldiers. But she is very glad that they do. She suddenly has more hope that it is going to be fine, that they are going to be okay. But she knows that the gods need to be there with them. She has not seen the gods in a while. Actually, she has not even slept in the longest while, but she is not sleepy.

Thinking about it now, it worries her. She has lost her concept of time, and this really bothers her now. She is not sure how long she has been in the Otherworld, and this suddenly disturbs her, because she has no clue about what is going on in the real world.

But she has nothing to worry about. Not that she knows it, but still. The thing with the Otherworld is that time is largely irrelevant. It does not matter how long it seems that you have been in the Otherworld, even if it feels like you have been here for days, barely a few hours will have gone by on the real plane. So Cath has hardly been in the Other-world for a full day in real-time.

She has no idea of this of course. So this is becoming a problem for her. She starts to feel a mix of urgency and anxiety that is very uncomfortable for her. She is distracted from the battle's preparations suddenly, looking around to see where the gods are. Again she keenly anticipates them, even Oenghus, who has made no secret of his love for her.

She thinks of the complicated situation that she now finds herself in. Confused, she knows she has no choice. Cath wonders what would have happened if Dagda had insisted on his love for her if he had fought his son. Then there would probably not be a vein of hope for her people. Quietly she is grateful for the way that things have turned out.

Cath again returns her focus to the matter at hand. She practices fiercely, determined to make a success of this expedition. There is nothing she can do about the way things have unfolded, but she can at least ensure that her people survive this onslaught. She can have a part to play in her people's survival.

She looks around again for a sign of the gods but sees nothing. Eventually, she puts down her swords and just throws herself on the grass. It is softer than any earth that she has ever felt before, and yet it feels strangely warm and comforting. She is tired but still has no need to sleep.

Cath feels the soft grass between her fingers and then digs them into the soft earth. She holds it up to the light and it shimmers. The beauty of it escapes her, her mind racing with thoughts of home. Just then Cath looks up to find herself surrounded by nymphs.

"You've been summoned," a nymph says, with a giggle in her voice. Cath almost thinks that there is something that they are not telling her. She gets up and follows them through a meadow that she does not remember seeing before. Then she remembers how everything changes shape in the Otherworld. She had almost forgotten the spectacular backdrop to her predicament.

She is in front of the gods again. Nervous, she looks at her hands, so that she is not sure of which gods are in front of her. She has seen Dagda, and Oenghus. Dewi and Epona are also present. As is Eochu, Dagda's brother. Some others too are present, but Cath does not see who.

Epona speaks. "So, how are preparations coming along for the day of battle?"

"I fear that we might be leaving it too long..." Cath speaks honestly.

"Too long, my dear?" Epona is calm, speaking with complete authority.

"Yes, too long. I can't even be sure if the battle isn't already over... but still we practice... still we..." Cath is clearly becoming more anxious.

"Things around you are not as they seem, my dear. You really have nothing to worry about." Epona speaks with a calm that seems to take over Cath too so that she is relaxed; despite the inner turmoil she is experiencing.

"But..." Cath starts.

"Now, now my dear, listen to me. Soon we will leave the Otherworld, for your world. We will be on the field of battle, and we will fight beside you against your enemies. But one thing must be made expressly clear, today, here, and now!" Epona raises her hand while she speaks so that Cath knows better than to interrupt her.

"After the battle is won, and your people are safe, you will return with us to the Otherworld. It will be your new home, and Oenghus will be your husband!" She says this so matter-of-factly that Cath could not protest if she wanted to.

The other gods present have nothing to add. Epona has said everything that this meeting was meant to cover. She has laid the conditions bare under which the gods will help Cath and the Celts. They just look to her for a response.

Oenghus too looks at Cath more intently. He really wants her to love him, but he knows that it is not really possible right now. She has too much on her mind, and her heart is still heavy with the totality of everything that she will be giving up. But he wants her here, back in the Otherworld, where he hopes to convince her once and for all of his love, and where he hopes she too can love him the same way one day.

This proposition settles over her like a dream. She does not even feel herself responding to anything the gods have said. Epona's voice is ringing in her head so that she feels like she is stuck inside a massive ringing bell, the toll of every dong shaking her to her core. She will return here, to this strange, wonderful, and beautiful place, and be the wife of a god.

How could this have happened? How could she be in this mess? She needs a moment to process everything but she does not feel like she has a moment. Everything seems to be happening all at once, and everything around her seems to be shifting and merging into one another so that nothing is clear anymore.

She slips in and out of lucidity, and the gods come in and out of focus. Eventually, she stops even trying to see them, and she stops trying to make out who is who. Cath just lowers her head and closes her eyes. Even with her eyes closed, however, she feels like she has them wide open, seeing everything like a dream, the kind that it seems that she will never wake from.

Oenghus fixes his gaze on her. He tries to see into her eyes, but they are closed. He wishes that she would open them, just for a moment, so that she can see the love that hangs so heavily in his. Nothing! She just keeps her head bowed low, her eyes shut tightly.

He wants to go to her, to hold her, and let her know that everything is going to be okay. But he can't. He just has to sit on his throne and observe. There is nothing that he can do, but just watch her being watched by the others. He knows that she is uncomfortable. He knows that she is anxious. But there is nothing that he can do about it.

Cath starts to process everything that has just happened. Everything suddenly seems to fall into some sort of order in her head. It suddenly feels like the veil has been lifted from her eyes and she sees everything very clearly now.

It is clear to her that she will never see her family again after the day of battle. It is clear that her life will never be the same again after the battle. It is clear that any sort of happiness is not in her future, not anymore. But this is a sacrifice that she has to make.

The realization that she will not be able to stay with her family again after the gods help them win the war settles over her in waves. It is not confusing though, like with the realization that she is not going to get to marry Eogan. It is just as though everything around her is suddenly clear, and irreversible.

Cath walks away in front of the gods, unable to look at them. She wanders into the meadow, and even the nymphs keep their distance. They continue to follow her, mind you, but not too closely. They seem to understand that she needs to be alone, and that again, she might need to cry. So they just follow her cautiously, watching her, and waiting to see what she might do next.

A mist settles over the Otherworld so that it seems like night has fallen. Cath knows somehow that this is not the case. The mist envelops her completely like the hug of a loved one so that she feels warm and comforted in spite of herself. She curls up on the earth and holds herself, rocking herself gently, willing herself to sleep.

She cannot though, no matter how hard she tries. So she just closes her eyes and continues to move herself backward and forward. The nymphs come in closer now, close enough to touch her but they don't. They just look at her curiously.

The gods are content with themselves. They have a long, subdued conversation about the coming wedding, not at all concerned about the battle. They trust that their soldiers will win against the Greeks and Romans. So they focus on the aftermath when Oenghus will have the prize, a new bride, a human bride.

It is very rare for someone to cross over to the Otherworld. The gods know this, and they are very pleased that one of them opened the porthole for this particular human. Nobody is saying who by the way. They just look at each other suspiciously, without asking any questions.

As quickly as it settled over them, the mist lifts. It feels strangely like morning, although Cath is sure that she has not slept. Still, she feels as though she has, which is a good thing. It is good because she can focus on the preparations, once again underway. But Cath has lost the sense of urgency, she has lost the anxiety she felt.

Time really is of no consequence here, she accepts. She knows that when they are deemed ready by the gods, they will be ready, and then they will make it onto the field of battle in time. She just has to trust that. There is nothing else that makes sense to her. She just has to believe this.

She watches as the soldiers of the Otherworld battle with each other, shifting from Greeks to Romans to Celts. It is a remarkable sight, and she has to almost pinch herself to bring herself back to the reality of what is happening. She has to focus on what lies in her immediate future, and the fact that she will at least help her people win this war. At least the gods have afforded her that opportunity, to see her home for the last time.

Soon enough, she is waving her sword like the best of

the soldiers on the field. She throws herself into the practice so that her mind is focused on one thing, winning. She cannot bring herself to even think about coming back to the Otherworld or marrying Oenghus. She is determined not to think about this.

Practice takes on a new meaning for Cath now. She knows in her heart that seeing Eogan and her father will be hard. But she also knows that there will be no time to focus on that. She will be slaying Greeks and Romans, secretly hoping that one of them slays her. Life after the battle without Eogan, or her father, will be unbearable.

Knowing that they are there, just beyond the scope of her new reality will be too much for her. She will not be able to deal with that, she feels. It will be better to die on the field of battle than to come back here after the war is over.

Oenghus too is torn. He knows that Cath's heart is not here with him. He watches her, seeing the fire inside her as she gets ready for the war. He wishes that she could burn with as much fire for him. But he tells himself that he just needs to be patient. Once the battle is over and the Celts are safe, Cath will see that everything that he did was for her.

It was Oenghus who opened up the way for Cath to end up in the Otherworld. He was curious about her and drawn to her beauty. His curiosity soon became love, until it raged inside him like an uncontrollable inferno. There is no turning back for him now. After the battle, he will make Cath love him. He just has to.

Dagda too has a lot on his mind. His son is going to be married to a woman that he himself had wanted. He had in fact pursued Cath, albeit secretly. This has been a strangely invigorating process; reminding him of feelings that he had mostly forgotten. But he has had to put his son's happiness before his own.

He wonders how he can get Cath to actually want to be with Oenghus. Never before has his son been so smitten. He's had his share of nymphs, and his pick of the goddesses. But he hasn't shown as much interest in them as he has shown in Cath. Dagda knows that she will make him happy. But he also knows that she will only be able to do this if she wants to.

Dagda looks at the soldiers as they prepare for the war that is so close now that you can smell the blood on the battlefield. There is excitement in the camp so that nobody even notices that he is among them. But as soon as they see him, everyone goes silent.

Cath too is silent. She looks up at Dagda and listens intently to what he has to say. He just looks at them as they fall in line, rows and rows of soldiers that suddenly form perfect squares. Even the gods who have been practicing on their own have come to this gathering.

Dagda takes his place on a podium that seems to have appeared out of nowhere. Everyone looks up at him now, so that their place in the hierarchy of the Otherworld is obvious. He looks over the vast crowd and utters the words that Cath has waited a million forevers to hear.

"We're ready!"

CHAPTER 11

CATH'S CHOICE-THE SPOILS OF WAR

THE GODS now prepare to leave the Otherworld. There is a tension in the atmosphere, however, because the gods very rarely get involved in human affairs on this level. There is no turning back now, however, and so everyone looks forward to the battle that is about to go down.

Cath paces the space between the trees of the grove that she finds herself in now. The nymphs have prepared her as best they can for the war ahead, and she looks every bit like a warrior princess again. She feels like a warrior too, and this shows in how she carries herself.

This does not take away the fact that she is nervous, however. She thinks of what she will do when sees Eogan, or her father. There will be no time for her to speak to them, and she cannot help but think that she may not even see them at all. Everything seems to have come together for her, however, and she is grateful.

Back home Eogan also paces. He walks the length and breadth of his house, holding in his hand the piece of paper that Ailill handed him the night before. It is a declaration of war. The Greeks and Romans are coming. They will meet on the field of battle in one day.

Eogan is not nervous about the battle. He knows that he will fight with everything that he has to protect his home. He is troubled by the last meeting that they had with the Druids and seers. Their final words still echo in his head: *It is all up to the gods now*!

From these words, Eogan can only assume that every possible outcome is possible. He has no choice but to believe this. There is nothing to lose really for him now, but still, he has a little bit of apprehension. He decides to take this apprehension with him onto the field of battle at dawn tomorrow.

Ailill looks over the settlement from his vantage point on one of the hills. He can see clearly across the entire span of it, and he finds himself humbled by what they have managed to do here. There is nobody in the streets now, no children playing in the meadows, no farmers in the fields.

He looks at the chimneys, and very few even have smoke coming out of them. He wonders what the people must be eating, probably just fruit and nuts. He can only imagine what they must be thinking. There is a strange calm now over the settlement, a calm that belies the obvious situation.

Eogan meets Ailill on the hill. It is easy to find him since he is the only one outside. He brings his horse up beside him and casts his eyes across the land. A thick silence settles between them, but both men know exactly what the other one is thinking.

They watch now as the men start to come out of their homes, armed and ready for war. The men gather around the base of the hill that they are on. They look at them, waiting for them to speak the words that will send them into the battle motivated.

Everything is silent now. Everything is still. All eyes are on Ailill and Eogan. The other generals have joined them now, as well as the Druids and some of the seers. Ailill looks at the old men, hoping that they will start speaking. He has not found the words yet that the men in front of him need to hear.

These men are also silent, however. Everyone is just looking to Ailill for instruction and guidance. Eventually, he has come out of his lull, realizing that this is probably the most important speech that he will make since their arrival on the Welsh Plain.

"Celts... the enemy is on our doorstep!" Ailill starts, not sure what the words are that will come out of his mouth, but also knowing that it cannot be forced or contrived. The men in front of him will notice this immediately.

"We must fight for what we have built here. We must fight for our families. We must fight for our lives. We must fight!" Ailill ends his speech with this admonition, and it resonates with his audience. Everyone has their helmet in their hands now, holding it to their chest. They look at the moon, sitting high now in the night sky. They need to get a good night's sleep in order to be ready for tomorrow.

The gods are ready too, standing on the threshold that separates the real world from the Otherworld. They make final adjustments to their armor, and they get their motivation right. Dagda gives them a final word of warning, not to use their powers in the real world, in full view of the human race. They know all of this, but still, Dagda needs to make sure.

It is as though he is the father of very unruly children. In essence, he is. They are excited by the possibilities that lie just beyond the threshold, and this excitement is almost palpable. You can almost smell it in the air.

He takes stock of every soldier that is going to accompany them to the other side. They are not equal in numbers to the combined forces they are about to face, but they stand taller than most of the soldiers waiting for them on the other side. They also have the element of surprise on their side as well.

Dagda walks through the rows of soldiers and gods alike. He gets to Cath, who is standing almost as tall as the men to her left and her right. She is a couple of rows in at the insistence of the gods. This is for her own protection, to make sure that she has soldiers all around her at any time.

After ensuring that all of them are ready, he prepares the porthole that will see them on the real plane. It takes him a few seconds, but it seems to take hours. Cath watches in amazement as Dagda conjures up a gateway out of nowhere. It is quite a spectacle.

The gateway opens up in midair. There are sparkles, and then stars, and then a strange, purple haze that forms a circle that gets bigger and bigger. It is a rather beautiful sight. Cath cannot turn her eyes from it. There have been few things as beautiful in their simplicity in the Otherworld.

Cath wonders why she did not see the same spectacle when she crossed over from the real world. Perhaps it is that every god creates a different gateway; one that is specific to their powers, or to their position in the Otherworld.

It is almost time for them to cross over. Cath is starting to get more and more anxious. There really is no turning back now though. They all brace themselves for the crossing, none of them more than Cath. She wonders where they will come out on the other side, and she almost hopes that she does not come out face to face with Eogan.

On the real plane, it is almost dawn. The Greeks and Romans are awake already, as are the Celts. Preparations have started in both camps for the war that will be well underway shortly after first light. Firstly, though, they have to have breakfast. Then they need to get their last bit of motivation from their leaders.

The Greeks and Romans are arrogant. They have such confidence in their victory that they speak as though they have already won. Their soldiers are prepared for this, more so than the Celts, and this shows in the way they carry themselves, and in the things that they say.

The Celts are as prepared as they are going to be. They have marched towards the field of battle already, a large sentry left behind to protect the settlement from any troops that break through the formations of battle and decide to attack the helpless left behind in it.

Upon arrival on their side of the battlefield, they start separating into their various formations. They all look to where Ailill has gathered with his generals, Eogan at his right hand. Once they are in position, they wait in keen anticipation for the final words of encouragement that will come from Ailill.

Ailill rides his horse up and down in front of his troops. He looks strong, and he sits high on his horse, looking confident and together. It really is do or die now for the Celts, and he knows this. He musters up every ounce of courage within him, putting all the strength inside of him on his face so that the troops in front of him see a strong leader in him.

"Our time has come! They say that many of us will fall today, but we cannot believe that. They say that it is up to the gods, and I say that the gods do not get to decide whether we live or die. We have to really reach within ourselves, and find courage and strength to fight, really fight, for everything that we hold dear." Ailill cannot come up with anything else to say, but no more is necessary.

The Celts' horses are becoming restless, almost as though they know something that the Celts do not. They know what this means. It means that there is something coming, something big. The Celts anticipate that the Romans and Greeks will come over the horizon at any moment. They hear nothing yet though, and so they know that it will be a while before the armies appear.

In the Greek and Roman camps, the soldiers have started to move. Thousands of men on horseback make for the Celtic settlement. They ride in silence, slowly making their way towards the Celts, determination on their faces. Each of them burns with the desire to see the enemy fall, and they have resolved to have as much fun doing it as possible.

Not once do they break formation. Perfect squares move uniformly behind thousands and thousands of foot soldiers. It is clear that they have one thing on their minds, and this clarity translates to their every movement. The horses too seem to move as one, so that it is as though a massive wave of soldiers is making its way across the Welsh Plains, to where the Celts are waiting for them.

Steadily the Roman and Greek contingent make their way towards the Celts. They move slowly and purposefully, in no hurry to get onto the field of battle. They are so confident of victory that they have become particularly nonchalant. There is no rush and no need for them to tire out their horses or themselves.

It is a short distance between the two armies mind you, but you would never guess it. The Celts stand ready all the same. Ailill has said everything that he is going to say to them. The other generals have nothing to add to what he has already said. They wait now, wait to see the enemy coming over the horizon, waiting to engage with them on the field of battle, waiting for whatever eventuality the gods deem fit.

There are about 20 000 Celtic soldiers. The odds are really against them, they know this. Actually, the only people that are aware of the odds are Ailill, his generals, the messengers, the Druids, and the seers. Everybody else is ignorant of this fact. It was very important that nobody else knows of the size of the army coming. It would be nearly impossible to keep up their morale if they did.

The Celts, therefore, are mostly oblivious to the magnitude of the threat coming, and so they keenly anticipate it. Their leaders just have to hope that the armies coming will not wipe them out too quickly. At the very least, the Celts must take down a number of men equal to their own numbers. Anything more would be seen as a blessing.

Ailill tries not to bow his head. He prays with his eyes to the heavens, therefore. There is no other way for him to consult with the gods one last time. He must however make this effort to entreat them once more, hoping in his heart that his request for assistance is heard.

What could they have done to disappoint the gods so, that it seems now they have been neglected, abandoned? This makes no sense to Ailill. Have they not observed every festival? Have they not shown gratitude for all the good things that the gods have done for them? Do they not praise the gods daily?

This seems so strange to Ailill that he cannot wrap his head around it. There is one thing that is clear to him, however, and that is that the forces of Rome and Greece are approaching them. They are approaching them quickly, it seems to the Celts, although they have not yet laid an eye on the massive oncoming army.

Time, however, is not on his side, so he cannot worry too much about what the gods will or will not do. He must focus on the military prowess of the men under his command right now because there is no time for anything else. There is time for just one thing on his mind right now, and he makes the conscious decision to focus on the parts of this situation that are under his control.

He rides the length of his own army now, and silently watches all of them, mostly on horseback, some foot soldiers. He really cannot think of anything else to say to them now, and he does not want to say anything that might distract them from the task. They appear slightly edgy now, and he knows that this means that they are amped for the battle ahead. He decides, therefore, to give them the space that they need to gather themselves.

This is the time that they need, mind you. They all go into themselves, digging deep in that place where they know that they have to do the best that they can if there is to be any hope of them to come out of this alive. They reach deep within themselves and pull out the last ounce of courage that lies hidden there. The effort from this starts to show on their faces, and they look even more confident of victory, more self-assured, and they stand just that much taller.

Eogan stands taller too, despite his broken heart. There is an almost palpable sadness now; it fills him so that he is forced to bring himself back to the present moment. Thinking of Cath will do him no good given the circumstance so that he has to just believe that she is safe. To believe anything to the contrary is simply too much for him right now.

Meanwhile, the armies are getting closer. Still invisible to them, but they can hear them approaching. The sound of their horses' hooves hitting the earth reverberates like a drum. This drumming gets closer still, even though they still have not seen them, despite their lookouts posted almost on the edge of the horizon.

The earth shakes now so that the Celts' horses become restless. They walk a few steps this way, and a few steps that way. Some of them come up on their hind legs now, so the riders need to reign them in. They manage to control their steeds, however. There is a tension now in the camp, a tension that they cannot ignore. Still, they appear confident so that this inspires confidence in the others around them, especially those who are not feeling so sure of themselves currently.

They face outwards now because they do not know where the sound is coming from. There is an increased nervousness, one that comes from the fact that they don't know where the threat is going to come from first. The protocols of battle insist that they engage via messenger first, however, but this seems unlikely to the Celts now. Nothing about this battle or the armies approaching them makes sense. Why then, would they follow even this most basic protocol now that they have come to plunder and destroy? Even the note that they received was a mere courtesy, the Celts feel.

The Greeks and Romans have made a steady advancement toward the waiting Celts now, and they are very close to them. Still, they are invisible to the Celts, so that they are increasingly nervous. The sun hangs in the sky now though, so that there is a shimmer in the distance that gives an indication of the oncoming masses.

They are formidable, it seems if the sea of silver light is anything to go by. The Celts strain to see just how many men are coming, but they cannot. It is still impossible for them to make out just how many soldiers are making their way toward them.

Things are getting very uneasy in the Celtic camp now so that they know that at any moment now they will see the enemy over the horizon, and meet them face to face on the battlefield. There is nowhere to run now, even if they wanted to and so the Celts start to steady and steel themselves for the battle that is now minutes away.

Nobody speaks to anyone now, the Celts are quiet. They look down at the earth and watch how this dust lifts off the ground now as the horses of the opposing army make their approach. They are trying not to show it, but now they are well and truly nervous, a mixture of anxiety and excitement. Any moment now, the enemy will come over the horizon, and at any moment now, the Celts will be in the worst battle of their lives.

CHAPTER 12

THE GREEK and Roman armies start to spill over the hills on the horizon, like the waves of the sea. The Celts no longer need to strain to see them now. They are clearly visible. Flashes of silver are caught by the early morning sunlight, and it just does not stop. They are literally spilling over the hills now, and although their approach is slow and steady, they are clearly on their way.

The Celts watch this approach, and they hold their horses steady. There is no escape for them now, but escape is not even on their minds. They are prepared to fight and fall for the life they have built here. Every single Celt on the battlefield has determined in their minds that they will not be taken alive and that if they are to fall, then this is the day that they will, this is the place that will fall, on their home soil. Their blood will soak their fields, they decide, but not until they have brought down their fair share of enemy soldiers.

Back in the settlement, the people gather together in the larger houses. They fortify them as best they can against possible attack, armed inside them, ready for anything that dares to enter the safety that they have created for themselves. They do not feel safe, however, and they are growing more and more anxious with every minute that passes.

The people huddle together, women with their children to their bosoms. The older couples too embrace, and husbands stand at the side of their families, their hands on their wives' shoulders, or their children's heads. They hold their slashing swords tightly with their free hands and plant their feet firmly into the floor. They fix their eyes on the only entrances to their respective houses and wait. It is the longest wait of any of their lives.

The women and some of the older children pray. They petition the gods for protection. They ask this both for themselves and for the men that are out on the battlefield. They are resolved within themselves to fight as well though, and they are determined that they will not go easily. The tension and anxiety pass through them like a dark shadow. Nobody, however, says anything that will give away how he or she really feels inside.

Meanwhile, on the battlefield, collision is imminent. The Greeks and Romans have suddenly picked up their pace, and they gallop steadily towards the waiting Celts. The Celts wait, buying their time. They wait, uncertain if the armies are going to stop, and unsure if they are going to first engage with their generals, as the protocol requires them to do. It becomes clear though that they will not, and so the Celts release their slashing swords from their pouches and raise them high above their heads. They look to Ailill now and wait for the order to attack.

Ailill's sword too is now free from its leather casing. He looks over his army, small in comparison, but no less formidable. He knows that they have no chance of success here, but he also knows that they will give it their all. He feels the need to say something, but he can see in their faces that all they want to hear is an order to attack.

There is no time for him to put together a sentence now, the armies closer now than ever. They are minutes from collision, seconds even. Ailill takes a deep breath and looks out over his warriors one last time. Then he turns his horse and faces the onslaught. He raises his sword higher now, and screams '*attack*', as he starts to gallop out in front of his soldiers.

The Celts follow suit, hearing the one word they have been waiting for. They have iron-sharp focus now, catching the frontline of enemy soldiers, and then catching at least ten rows into their formations. The rest of them just seem to merge in a tan and red band, with flashes of silver that make them look like a huge forest fire.

Each man goes into his own mind suddenly and focuses on his own targets. Three, four, five Greeks and Romans for every Celt on the frontline, clear in their periphery. They don't even see the other Celts on the battlefield anymore, so clear is the focus. There is no turning back, no turning away as the armies collide. The two forces mesh together and become one as steel meets steel. The battle is really now in full swing.

Cath's father is fearless, and very quickly he has pierced twenty men in their sides. Shortly thereafter, twenty more have fallen, and Ailill has not even broken a sweat yet. Eogan fights as fiercely too, bringing many Greeks and Romans down very quickly. The Celts really seem to have started the battle off on the right foot, and the frontlines of the enemy are breached very quickly.

The Celts fight with a determination that they never thought they were capable of. Every man fights for his family, and this lights a fire in him so that they start to make easy work of the Greeks and Romans. It doesn't last long, however.

The onslaught is relentless. The enemy just keeps on coming and coming, and the Celts start to tire out. Even Ailill is beginning to tire. There are just so many of them, and it catches many of the Celts by surprise. It starts to look very bad for them, as they start to weaken more and more.

They try, though, and keep bringing themselves back into the thick of things. Resilience is something that the Celts have in buckets, but it starts to look like it is going to fail them. They start to fall, one by one, and then they start to fall quickly so that soon enough the only Celts left on the frontline are Eogan and Ailill. Still, these two press forward, making inroads into the enemy attack. They are now completely surrounded by Greeks and Romans, but they make them quickly regret clashing swords with the Celtic leaders.

The Celtic army is taking serious losses now, but neither Ailill nor Eogan can think about this right now. In fact, every one of them, foot soldiers and generals alike, has just one thing on their minds, and one thing only. So those with an ounce of strength left to fight on, spurred on by the thought of their families, and the fate that awaits them if the enemy crosses the battlefield and enters the settlement.

Then suddenly, just as it starts to seem that all is lost, the army suddenly doubles in size. Still, the Celts don't notice. The Greeks and Romans on the other hand, are a different cases altogether. Suddenly they seem to be surrounded by more Celts so their complacence is shaken. At first, they think they are seeing things, but soon enough the steel from their blades confirms their reality.

The gods have started to cross over from the Other-world, and their timing could not have been better. They come out of thin air, onto the field of battle, and replace the fallen Celts. The wounded men are carried off the battlefield. They are taken care of by some seers who have been watching from the sidelines. These men have noticed the sudden expansion on the battlefield, but they cannot be sure where they come from.

The sun is high in the sky now, so that everyone who notices that there are suddenly more Celts on the battlefield is not sure if it is just their mind playing tricks on them. The only ones who are sure that these ghosts are real are the Greeks and Romans falling at the hand of their swords. Even the Celtic seers are putting it down to the fact that they are not caught in this battle, so they cannot know how many soldiers are actually on the field.

Even when the army triples, the only people that are really aware of this are the enemy army. There is confusion now on the battlefield, and everyone is focused on the soldiers in front of them. There is no time for them to even look around, to even think of anything other than staying alive and fighting for their home.

The gods and their warriors are having a very good time. They really enjoy the confrontation and the swordplay. It is really played to them, and they are more than a match for the Greeks and Romans. Swords clash, steel against steel, the base of the swords held firmly in their grip. And when swords fall to the earth, the gods and their warriors resort to fists.

It really is a brilliant battle. Swords slice through Celts, and they fall to the earth. When they slice through the god's warriors, they make no impact. The Greeks and Romans are confused, and this confusion shows on their faces. Even the swords in enemy hands start to tremble, and some of them lose their grip.

The gods and their warriors start to overtake the Celts in the battle. They make their way to the front of the battle lines, and start to make good work of the opposition. The Celts are grateful for the relief, and they don't even notice that they do not recognize the extra men now fighting with them. It is probably their helmets, but soldiers move in a specific way, a sort of signature. The Celts do not recognize the movements of these men who now fight with them.

Ailill is still in the front of the battle, however, and so is Eogan. They fight on valiantly, even though just a few seconds ago they were on the losing end of this war. They both notice one warrior in particular, not Greek, not Roman. This soldier does not even move like a man. It can't be however, they think.

Looking closer, however, they both recognize the movements, the style of this warrior. She is a princess, a Celtic princess on the battlefield with them. Ailill is convinced that he is seeing things. His daughter is safe in Scotland somewhere, away from all this madness. She is sitting by a loch, high in the Scottish highlands, thinking of him, missing him.

Eogan, too, watches this warrior princess more closely. He is sure that he is just seeing what he wants to see. He remembers all the conversations he had with Cath before she left, about how she would fight for her people. How she would fight with her people. This cannot be her, here on the field of battle, close enough for them to touch if there were not so many Greeks and Romans between them. Both men return their focus to the battle at hand.

The heat under her mask becomes too much for her, and after bringing down a few more Romans, Cath removes the heavy metal case. Her hair suddenly blows up in a gust of wind as her braids come undone. The sun catches every strand of her beautiful hair and kisses the side of her face so that it shimmers. Everyone on the battlefield close enough to notice her suddenly freezes.

Cath is the only one who is not distracted by her appearance. She manages to bring a few more Greeks and Romans down before they catch their breath and refocus. Suddenly, all of the enemies seem to come down on her. They want to kill her for the damage that she has done to them. They also want to capture her as a trinket that they can enjoy for a while before they kill her. This gives Cath another gap to cause even more damage to their infantry.

The enemy regains their composure, but just as quickly, they lose it again. Cath really is the kind of beauty that will distract even men of the strongest will. Each time they lose their focus, she is piercing through them with her swords. Every time their focus returns, men who will fight to the death to protect her surround Cath.

Two men in particular move closer and closer, determined to get close to the warrior princess. They have to be sure that their eyes are not in fact playing tricks on them. They need the certainty that will come only from looking at her face, into her eyes. They push through the soldiers standing between them and Cath, Romans, Greeks, and Celts alike. Both men do not even notice themselves fighting the enemy off with renewed determination.

Ten Romans are suddenly on Ailill. They are no match for his swordsmanship, however. Still, they cause enough of a delay in his advancement towards his daughter. Eogan seems to have a clear path towards her, though, and he takes advantage of this fully. He heads in Cath's direction, dropping more of the enemy's foot soldiers from his vantage point high on his horse. He just must get to Cath, and quickly.

He watches as Cath too fights skillfully, admiration filling his eyes where apprehension once sat heavy. She is really quite a vision to behold, determined and feisty. You cannot help but watch her. Eogan cannot keep his eyes off her. The soldiers that come upon him are just a distraction now, a mild irritation like some of the summer insects that buzz around your face when you try and sleep.

Eventually he is close enough to her to see the sweat on her brow. He watches it glistening down her face, settling on her nose. He tries to convince himself that this is all a dream, but then he is fighting off two Romans on horseback, and the reality of what is going on settles over him. He cannot really be looking at Cath though, he reasons.

Just then, Cath meets Eogan's eyes, and everyone around them suddenly disappears. There seems to be a haze over the Welsh Plains now, and the only two people on the battlefield are the two of them. They seem to be seeing each other for the first time, and old feelings feel strange and new. Eogan just wants to touch her. Cath wants nothing else but to be touched by them. They lose each other in each other's eyes for what seems like the longest time.

Suddenly a spine-chilling curdling sound comes from just behind Cath so that she turns her head to see what it is, breaking the lock with Eogan. Oenghus has appeared, seemingly out of nowhere, and brought down a Greek soldier who was moments away from beheading the Celtic princess. Eogan and Cath are pulled violently from their temporary lull, and they are back in the battle almost immediately.

They turn away from each other now, again facing down the Greeks and Romans that are determined to see their blood spill on the earth. There is no time for thoughts of love anymore. They have to focus on the task. Both

Oenghus and Eogan are not too far from Cath anymore, however. They are both determined to protect her at all costs. They fight with renewed vigor, Cath uppermost in both their minds, the mortal for his reasons, the god for his own. Both reasons are remarkably similar, though.

Eogan notices the looks that the god steals of Cath, and feelings start to stir inside him. Part anxiety, part jealousy, he suddenly has a million questions that he needs to ask Cath. This, however, is certainly not the place or time. He does wonder, however, amidst all the carnage, if such a time will ever come.

Oenghus too notices how Eogan looks at Cath. He notices how he protects her now, and how he fights every possible threat to her safety with a fierce determination that goes far deeper than mere self-preservation. He knows who he is, without being told. He hates him immediately and wishes secretly that a Greek or Roman sword pierces him soon.

He is, after all, human, Oenghus reasons. He cannot possibly hold out for too long. The army that has come to kill them is a large one, and it is only a matter of time before he tires out, and gives in to defeat. Even though he seems rather resilient, Oenghus is all too aware of the human condition, and he knows that it is only a matter of time before Eogan's body admits defeat, and he will be dead.

Then nothing will stand in his way, and Cath will truly be his. She is going to return to the Otherworld, that is the arrangement. With Eogan dead, however, Oenghus sees a way into Cath's heart. Something that would not be possible if she knows she left him alive behind. Oenghus keeps a closer eye on Eogan now.

Both her suitors are side by side now, God and human, both hoping that this battle will be over soon. Eogan needs to speak to Cath, to hold her. Oenghus cannot wait to take her back to the Otherworld so that they can start their life together. Eogan too notices that there must be something going on with Cath and this man he does not know. He, too, wishes secretly that he falls on the battlefield so that any confusion in her heart can be eradicated.

They fight on, determined now, not just to keep Cath safe, but to be the only surviving man vying for her affection. A lot can be read in the way things unfold, and this situation proves it. None of them have spoken to the other, but they are all aware of the triangle web that they find themselves caught in. All three of them try not to think about this, but it is the only thing that they can think of.

They fight in their own worlds now, their own bubbles. The outcomes of this war are not guaranteed, but Eogan, Oenghus, and Cath all have their own hopes of how it will end. Eogan sees himself embracing Cath, with the enemy defeated. Oenghus sees Eogan fall, and he sees his return to the Otherworld with a woman by his side, and a wedding to plan. Cath has her own dreams of how this will end, but the reality of the situation keeps returning to her and overcoming her in constant relentless waves.

The battle rages on, with many Celts falling, but as many Greeks and Romans. The enemy count is dwindling, thanks mostly to the gods. They are really making quick work of the very large army that has come to destroy everything that the Celts have done on the Welsh Plains. It is early yet, too early for them to start doing any sort of victory dance, but it is going rather well for the gods, and they have yet to break even the slightest of sweats.

CHAPTER 13

THE CELTS WAGE the war with a verve that the Greeks and Romans didn't expect. Even when some of them fall, ten more seem to rise up, out of nowhere, and take their place. Still, the enemy battles on assured of the strength that they have in numbers. Surely the Celts cannot beat them. They know that there are no more than 20 000 men in the settlement's army. Even if there were 100 000, they would still outnumber them 3 to 1.

The thought of failure doesn't even cross their minds as they fight on. They have one mission, and one mission only. That is to completely annihilate the Celts, and wipe any trace of them from the pages of history. This mission spurs them on, even as more and more of their men fall by the way. Where the Celts are resilient, the Greeks and Romans are not lacking at all in determination, completely resolved to accomplish what they set out to accomplish.

Oenghus fights bravely, even cockily. He knows after all that he is a god, and that no Greek or Roman can do any sort of damage to him. He keeps on catching Eogan in his peripheral, especially when he seems to come too close to Cath. He fights his way to her until he again is by her side.

Eogan has no time to notice this, however. He is surrounded by a constant flow of attacking soldiers now so that he has no choice but to concentrate all his energies on the matter at hand. He musters up strength from deep within himself, and when he feels like his energy is waning, he reminds himself of why he is fighting. It works, and he is bringing down soldiers like he has just stepped onto the battlefield, fresh and vigilant.

Ailill has also worked his way to Cath, eventually. He fights back to back with his daughter, a million things that he wants to say to her, but he cannot at the moment. Cath is any man's equal with a sword, and she manages to fight with her father to bring some serious damage to the numbers on the other side. As the enemy surges upon them relentlessly, many more Celts fall, but the gods, Cath, Ailill, and Eogan seem to have the will to defend the Welsh Plains even more, with a determination that is impressive to see.

Back at the empires, the leaders do not know what is going on on the field of battle yet. They celebrate the expected victory, sure that there is no other outcome possible in this war. Their people too are feeling exceptionally celebratory, and many feasts break out in pockets all over Rome and Greece. Their arrogance is truly remarkable.

Women dance among the revelers, entertaining emperors and laymen alike. There are very large pigs spread out and stuffed with apples, and many traditional foods spread out across tables all over the land. The people stuff their faces, and what they do not eat, they throw to the waiting dogs, until even the dogs have had more food than they can take.

The wine flows freely among the men and women.

Many of them become rather amorous, and they give in to their lust. After all, there is much to celebrate, they feel. The fall of the Celts is a feather in the caps of both empires and they make no secret of the fact that they absolutely hate the Celtic people. Massive drunken orgies break out, with people making love in public open places. Women move between groups of men, giving themselves up to them willingly, festively almost. It is a wild hot mess of lust and hormones, and nobody is fighting their urges at all.

Their oracles are, however, caught in their own frenzy. They consult with their own omens, and the message that they are getting is not as clear as they would like it to be. Suddenly they are not as sure of victory as the people are, and so the Greek oracles send the temple princesses away from them so that they can continue with their divination.

One thing becomes particularly clear to them, and that is that they are suffering great losses on the battlefield. They expected some casualties, with the Celts being formidable opponents, but nothing like what they are being shown. To make matters worse, they cannot get any more men out to the battlefield anymore, the Welsh Plains a far distance from the Greek Isles.

The oracles seek out the emperor, who is on top of one woman, with many more around him, all anxiously waiting their turn with the virile man. They cannot wait for him to finish his current conquest, needing to speak to him as a matter of the highest urgency. However, what he can do about the information that they bring is very little.

The emperor, however, does not dismount. He continues to thrust violently until after some time he is eventually satisfied. He rolls off her, leaving her breathless. He is surprised to find that he is surrounded by the old wise men of Greece but doesn't ask them to leave, the look on their faces letting him know that what they have to say cannot possibly wait.

"Leave us!" the emperor instructs the women, who are all over the room and bed, naked, waiting.

"What is it that cannot wait until..." he starts to ask as the room empties.

"We have had visions!" The oracles all seem to speak at the same time.

"Yes, yes, what is it?" He is agitated and keen to get back to his carnal activities.

"It does not go well for us on the Welsh Plains!"

"Some casualties are to be expected...this is war after all!" He cannot hide his arrogance. He sent over 150 000 of his best men to fight the Celts, whose army was considerably smaller, so he has no reason not to be so sure of himself.

"This is more than just a few casualties. We fear that they might be getting help from divine sources!" The oracles try to speak as clearly as they can, the emperor looking at them with a confused gaze.

"What kind of help? From the gods? Where are our gods? Why don't our gods help us?" He is suddenly very nervous, the men in front of him looking very serious indeed.

"We have not asked for any help..."

The Greek oracles caution against enthusiasm, still unclear about the extent of the damage that the Celtic gods are exacting on their soldiers. They advise the emperor to send word to Rome, which he does immediately. He knows that his sense should have been to consult with the gods of Greece before they set out on this mission. It is too late now, and he can do nothing but hope for the best.

The Romans are having their own festivals, mind you.

Wild orgies play out in the houses, and in the streets. The wine flows easily, and freely. The Roman leaders have organized very elaborate shows, their gladiators killing each other for the amusement of those who are not having wild and uninhibited sex. This is truly a premature celebration of victory, but how can they know what is happening on the Welsh Plains, with no word yet from the battlefield, the battle barely a half a day in.

The sun shines down on the lands of Greece and Rome, and even on the Welsh Plains. The atmosphere in these three lands, however, is very different. On the Welsh Plains, the battle is in full force. Blood is spilling from both sides of the battle lines, but significantly on the side of the Greeks and Romans. In Greece, there is suddenly concern amongst the leadership, with the words that the oracles have spoken. Rome is caught in a massive festival, celebration filling the air even though they have no idea what is happening on the field of battle.

Back in the Welsh Plains, it is red. Bodies are carried off the battlefield as they fall, just to make space for the fighting soldiers to move. What the Greeks and Romans had thought would be easy has turned out to be anything but. They suffer major losses, and it seems that they are unable to penetrate the now solid line formed by the gods. The Celtic humans are having a chance to catch their breath, not sure where these reinforcements came from but appreciating them nonetheless.

Eogan and Ailill are still on the frontlines, however. So are Cath and Oenghus. Dagda has also made an appearance. He is truly the most vigilant warrior on the field. His sword cuts through four or five Romans at once, and then four or five Greeks. None of the gods have even thought of using their powers yet though, and there is a certain arrogance to them, each and every one of them, that shows in how they confidently wield their swords.

Cath, Eogan, and Ailill are the only humans in the front of the battle now, but they too get a reprieve as the gods and their warriors fight back the enemy with formidable force. Oenghus however, still has his eyes on Eogan, hoping beyond hope that he will at any minute fall at the hand, or sword, of an enemy. It does not happen, however, the gods very diligently protecting each of the three human beings.

Oenghus works his way to beside Eogan, eventually. They are eventually side-by-side, and the god feels like he should just pierce him himself, and end this game. He knows however that this is not possible, not with the deal that the gods made with Cath.

Ailill and Cath are behind the front line now, Cath exhausted and Ailill needing to check that she is okay. He removes his helmet and looks at his daughter, looking every bit like any of his warriors, but still managing somehow to look like his little girl. He wants to take her in his arms, and take her away from this battle. He has tried that before, however, and he knows that it will not work. Nothing will stop Cath from helping her people.

He cannot come up with the words to articulate the questions that he has for her, also needing to catch his breath. He is also just so happy to see her, that the context of their reunion is suddenly irrelevant. Eventually, he cannot help himself, reaching out, and touching her face. She is real. Everything that is happening now is very real. Ailill almost cannot believe it.

Suddenly they both look up, hearing an agonizing cry somewhere near the front. Cath knows immediately who this is. Ailill too knows who the cry is coming from so that he is immediately reenergized, and making his way to the front of the onslaught. Cath disobeys her father again and follows him.

A Greek sword slices through Eogan, and then he lets out another cry as the owner of the sword pulls it from its new perch. Eogan falls to his knees, but just before the Greek can deliver the death blow, he is on the receiving end of Ailill's steel. Ailill swiftly separates this eager soldier and his head, and then he lets out a cry of his own.

He presses on, determined to avenge the damage that was done to his most trusted general. Ailill wields his swords with an almost passion now, as he looks over his shoulder, and screams for them to get Eogan off the battle-field. Before Cath can get to him, he is gone, removed swiftly from any further danger. Although, judging from his wounds, it might already be too late for him.

Cath watches as the Celts carry the man she loves off the battlefield. She tries to run to him, but Oenghus pulls her back. The look in his eyes says 'Remember the promise you made to us back in the Otherworld'! She has so many emotions going through her at once now, Eogan, Oenghus, and her father all forming pieces of a very elaborate puzzle inside her.

She loves Eogan. She knows this. She also knows that she made a promise to the gods, a promise that she must keep if her people are to enjoy their freedom and safety, and if she is going to ensure that they are kept safe going forward. She hates Oenghus, and all the gods, for their self-ishness, and their complete disregard for real human emotion.

Cath looks around at them, fighting just for the sake of fighting. They seem to be having the time of their lives, and this bothers her. It suddenly bothers her just how much they are enjoying the battle. They really have a taste for blood and an appetite for a war that she would not have thought possible back in the Otherworld.

Back in the Otherworld, they were all so carefree, playing tricks on each other and making love to beautiful nymphs, and having all their needs met. Now, she sees them as savage monsters who enjoy the sheer sport of killing. She knows that she asked them to help her out, that it is because of her that they are here. She cannot help but think, though, that perhaps it wasn't the best idea. Looking around at their own casualties, and at the soldiers being given a chance to recover, she knows that she did not have another choice.

She throws her eyes to where Eogan is being carried off, on the edge of the battlefield. Cath makes a choice to focus all her energies on the matter at hand, and grips her two slashing swords tighter. She makes an easy meal of ten more enemy soldiers, no longer seeing Greeks and Romans. All she sees is the reason why her life will never be the same again. This thought angers her and fuels her forward so that she is breaking through their formations fiercely, cutting through them almost blindly.

Her thoughts are no longer on her home, Eogan, or even her father. She has resolved to fall on this field today, once she is sure that her people have a chance of winning this battle. Cath is seeing red now, however, and making her presence felt on the battlefield. She has made peace with her own death already, but she is definitely in no hurry to die. She will kill as many of these bastards before she falls.

Ailill catches his daughter in his periphery. He watches her fighting, pride hanging heavy in his eyes. His focus cannot shift too much from the men aiming to kill him, however, and so he presses on with the battle. His power seems to be restored, and he too is in it to win it now. He scopes the battlefield once more, to gauge their losses. They are doing better than he could ever have hoped.

Cath's thoughts start to change again, and she is once again thinking of Eogan, injured or dead on the sidelines. She has to know if he is okay, or at least kiss him one last time if he is not. She can almost feel his lips on her own and taste his tongue. She seems to battle on in an automatic fashion now, her thoughts not on the fight before her anymore.

She cannot help herself and starts to move back from the frontline. She is still surrounded by the enemy, however, and they just keep on coming, but she is clearing the path for herself to where she thinks Eogan must be lying. Trying to fight the urge to go to where he is has been harder even than this battle, and she cannot do it. She just cannot avoid seeing the love of her life in his final moments.

The gods too watch her as she moves to where the injured man lies. Oenghus makes for Cath quickly. He must stop her. He cannot risk her changing her mind. There is an almost tangible love, even now, here amongst all this chaos, that is shared between Eogan and Cath. Nobody on the battlefield that sees them can deny this. Oenghus has got to get to Cath before she gets to Eogan.

They meet at last, and Oenghus grabs her hand. She almost expects to be whisked away to the Otherworld immediately, and so for a moment, just a moment, she closes her eyes. But then Oenghus comes in close to her and looks at her in her eyes. She cannot look at him, though, and she turns her head away from him.

"Don't do this!" he speaks in a loud whisper so that she is sure that everyone on the battlefield can hear them.

She has no response to this. There is nothing that she can say to him. They are suddenly surrounded by many of the god's warriors, protecting them while they are temporarily distracted from the events going on around them. Oenghus cannot himself think of what else to say to Cath, and he too for a moment wants to just open the portal to the Otherworld and drag Cath through it. The battle is still underway, however, and this is not an option. They have both made promises to each other, and he can only hope that she will keep to her end of the bargain.

Suddenly Cath looks at Oenghus, an '*I'm Sorry*' in her eyes. She pulls away from him and starts running to the last place she saw Eogan. He tries to follow her, tries to catch up with her. He can too, if his conscience hadn't started to bother him. Oenghus slows down and just watches Cath run across the battlefield.

Cath pushes past the men surrounding Eogan on the ground. He can't be dead, he just can't. She bends down and takes him in her arms, knowing at that very moment that she is breaking her promise to the gods and that there will probably be hell to pay for her choice. What other choice could she have had in the matter though, she wonders, and then she decides not to think about it. Her focus and energy must be on Eogan now, who is not doing too well, but at least he is still alive.

CHAPTER 14

THE GODS ARE INTRIGUED by human love, but they really don't have the time right now to be intrigued. They make the decision to continue to fight for the humans, even though Cath seems to have gone back on her promise to return with them. They are having too much fun anyway, so why stop now. They might as well finish this.

Oenghus too decides to continue in battle despite Cath's choice; there is nothing he can do to force Cath to love him. He does not want to. He wants her to really love him, from her heart, but her heart clearly belongs to Eogan. Oenghus cannot deny this. He lets his agony out through his sword and takes his frustration out on the Greeks and Romans.

Dagda watches as his son moves through the enemy soldiers with an anger he hasn't seen in a very long time. He wants to just take Cath with him back to the Otherworld and force her to keep her promise. Even he must admit though that it will be a fate worse than death for her, especially with what he has witnessed here on the real plane.

Human love is truly a complex emotion. Real human love is a beautiful thing to see.

The gods and their warriors replace every Celt now on the frontline, including Ailill. They move swiftly upon the enemy and start to drive them backward. There is no time for them to retreat, however, and more and more of them fall to the ground. There is not even time anymore to carry their dead off the field, as the gods obliterate them, swiftly and systematically.

Finally, they are evenly matched, one to one, god and warrior to an enemy soldier. The sun is starting to set over the horizon now, and the battle is almost over. The Celts have won, although they are still not sure how. All they know is that Cath, their beloved princess came at the last minute with reinforcements. The Celts are now the audience, and they watch as the warriors that came with Cath finish up the battle.

It is epic, what the Celts witnessed. The sun seems to be suspended now, hanging in its final position in the sky just before it gives way to the night. This last light serves to just allow the audience to see every detail of the last stages of the battle that wages on to its finality. The Celts cannot help being unable to believe what has just happened here. They cannot believe that in just one day, they have beaten an army that was so strong. Unsure of even how many Greeks and Romans there were, they just know that they were greatly outnumbered.

Now they can however see the end of this battle, and they cannot hide the fact that they are relieved. Ailill is impressed by the sheer showmanship of these warriors that Cath has blessed them with. He looks over to where she is still watching over Eogan who still has not regained consciousness. Cath feels her father's eyes on her, and she looks up to meet his gaze. His eyes say everything that is impossible for him to articulate in this moment, sheer gratitude and appreciation that she did not stay away.

He returns his looks to the armies in their final clash. Nobody is going to escape this field with their lives. Even though the attacking armies try to retreat, escape is just not possible. They too fight back with every last ounce of strength they have left in them, however, and this is admirable. Try as they might, however, they are no match for the gods, and their warriors, and soon enough the last of the Greeks and Romans falls to the ground. The sun finally sets.

They take a moment to take in this victory. Ailill knows that no matter what happens now, going forward, any army will think twice before they think about attacking the Celts. He doesn't anticipate even the suggestion of war going forward. All the Celts go down on their haunches and bow their heads low. They all thank the gods in silence and bid the dead farewell. They count the cost of this war, but they also count their blessings.

After they have all gathered themselves sufficiently, they start to congratulate each other. The dead are carried off; their families need to know about their losses. The gods and the warriors are already perfectly aligned again and awaiting instructions from Dagda and Oenghus. They cannot help but notice that Cath is no longer among them, however, and they all start to ask the obvious questions.

Dagda and Oenghus look at one another, not sure of what it is they want to say to each other, but knowing that something needs to be said. Dagda eventually pulls Oenghus away from the crowd now looking at them intently, and gathers his thoughts, so as to say the right thing to his son, who is obviously going through something that he has never experienced before.

"What do you want us to do now, son?" he asks, needing to put this in his court, letting him decide the way that he wants this to play out.

"Can we force her to go back with us?" Oenghus has to ask the question, even though this is something that he will never be able to even consider.

"We can!" Dagda says emphatically, "We are after all gods, and we can have anything that we want!"

"I know what I want father, but I also know what she wants...and it is not me!" Oenghus has to say it aloud so that he can hear it outside of his head. It hurts even more though, and he wishes he had not said it almost as soon as the words escape his mouth.

"We can take her back with us!" Dagda reiterates what he has already said, needing Oenghus to be clear as crystal about the options that he has.

"I don't want to be loved like that father!"

"Are you saying..."

"Yes, father, she must stay here, among her people, with him!" Oenghus searches for that place that is supposed to feel good inside, that place that knows that you are doing the right thing, making the ultimate sacrifice. He cannot find it. He wonders if it even exists, and if so, why he does not seem to possess this place within himself.

"Are you sure son?" Dagda asks, just to be certain.

"Yes, father, I am sure!"

"You will be a great leader of the gods one day my son!" Dagda feels the need to embrace his son, just to confirm how proud he is of him. He avoids this though, thinking that this will be too human an action for a god of his stature.

"Cath?!" Ailill has finally found himself standing next to his daughter.

"Father!" She comes up to him and throws her arms around him. There is no trace of his little girl left in her now. He sees her for what she is. She is now a woman, a warrior, a true Celtic princess. He cannot hide his tears anymore. There is no need to. They both weep, for joy mixed with relief. The whole world melts away now.

When everything comes back into focus, Cath starts to tell her father of her journey. She leaves nothing out. She is unable to. She even tells him that her horse is missing, lost somewhere in the Otherworld. He assures her that it is not lost, just wandering about, enjoying the strange wonder of this land that he has never seen. Cath describes it in such detail, however, that he feels like he was right there with her.

The Druids come over to where they stand, anxious, needing to talk with Ailill alone. Arrangements need to be made to dispose of the 300 000 bodies that litter the battle-field. Messages need to be sent to the Greeks and Romans. A festival to the gods needs to be planned, in thanks for everything that they have done for them.

"The gods are among us, we can personally thank them!" Ailill throws his eyes in the direction of the rows of warriors in such perfect alignment that they can only be from the Otherworld. The Druids wonder why they did not see this before, the seers too, but given the events of the day, they cannot really be too hard on themselves.

They check that Eogan is being taken good care of, and then Ailill gives instructions to burn every single body of the Greek and Roman troops that dared to come and chal-lenge them. Everybody sets about with the task that they have been assigned, even some of the other men and women from the settlement come up to help. They take care of the injured and help the wounded men home.

Ailill and Cath, along with the Druids and seers make their way to the gods, to thank them personally. The Druids want to make great pomp and ceremony, but Ailill tells them not to worry about it. He tells them not to think too much about the ceremony of everything, it is just important that the leader of the Celts speaks personally to the leader of the gods.

When they eventually get to the front of the rows of warriors, they seek out Dagda. Cath points him out to Ailill, too ashamed to stand before him now, remembering the promise that she made to them in the Otherworld. She remembers how passionately she pleaded with this very god, and how sincere she was when she promised them that she would return with them after the Celts had won the war.

Now, though, she has obviously changed her mind. She has not said this to the gods mind you, but they know. They can see it written all over her face. She will of course go back with them, if they insist, knowing that a time will come when her people need the protection of the gods again. She cannot risk her people losing favor with the gods just because she could not keep her promise.

There are ways to make this work for her, she knows. This is not the best thing for everyone concerned, however; there is no way that she can please everybody. The one person that is going to be most disappointed if she stays is Oenghus. She knows this. It is clear on his face, and Cath cannot bring herself to even look at him. She keeps her head bowed low, and hopes that her father starts speaking soon to ease the tension a little bit. Everything, anything, will be better than the cold silence that seems to be taking over across the field right now.

Instead of speaking so that everyone can hear him, though, Ailill asks to speak with Dagda privately. Everyone looks on as they make their way a little further up the hill, and look over the entire scene, brightly lit now by the fires that are already consuming the bodies of the Greeks and Romans. Nobody can hear what Ailill is saying to Dagda, or what Dagda says to Ailill. The conversation is obviously meant to be private.

"I cannot begin to thank you for everything that you have done for us here today. We will be forever indebted to you!" Ailill starts the conversation, in response to the look of anticipation coming from the god.

"We do what we must...about your daughter..." Dagda needs to know how much Cath has let her father into their secret world, and if she told him about the promise that she made.

"Please don't take her from me again...I would rather have died on the field today than lose her again!"

"She made a promise..."

"I know...I know...Surely there is some other way that we can make good on this promise, surely..." Ailill feels like he is talking too much because Dagda silences him by raising his hand.

"She will stay with you...but only because my son doesn't want to force her to love him. She is obviously in love with the young man who fell, although I cannot say that I understand it!"

"There are things in the Otherworld that I could never understand... Can we not just leave it at that?"

"Yes, I think it is best. Let us go back now, and you can show us this world you call home and let us see just what it is that we fought for!" Dagda leads out in front of Eogan as though he knows where he is going. He is so used to being the leader.

The gods are now chaperoned around the real world, and they look at everything with as much marvel as Cath had looked at everything in the Otherworld. Oenghus has still not been able to speak to Cath, but she feels like she needs to say something to him. So after she has summoned enough courage in herself, she approaches him cautiously.

"I'm sorry..." is all she manages, tears already streaming down her face.

"Don't do that...Don't cry...It's okay Cath, it really is!" Oenghus says the words quickly before they fail to come out of him. He holds Cath tightly, fiercely, knowing that he is holding her for the last time. "Go to him..."

She thanks him, and then leaves him to his own thoughts. He goes off with a couple of other warriors and distracts himself from his emotions with the spectacle that is the human beings that they are surrounded by. Cath goes off to find Eogan, tears still streaming down her face as she realizes everything that they have managed to do here today.

She finds him asleep in a tent on the edge of the battle-field. He is still too weak to move, and so they have made him as comfortable as they can make him given the circumstance. Everybody moves around, Celts and gods alike, everyone going through the motions now, the victory not yet settling over them. There is a clear sense of relief however among every single one of the Celts in the settlement and on the battlefield.

Ailill needs to speak to his people, but he also needs them to first recover sufficiently from the day's exploits. They really fought a good fight, every one of them. He knows this, and he knows that the Celts who lost their lives today did not fall in vain. He will have to speak to them soon though, but not just yet.

He rides the length and breadth of the settlement, tears of joy streaming down his face. He cannot let anybody see him so emotional, although the people might appreciate seeing the softer side to their leader. However, he really needs to be alone, and Ailill himself needs to process what has just happened here today.

Ailill comes upon the river that runs through the settlement, and he stops beside it and dismounts. He washes his face in the water, rushing by now as if it is clearing the settlement of the events of the day. He watches the water rushing by, with his sweat and his blood being carried away. Eventually, though, he just throws his whole body into the water and stays under the water for a long time.

He rejoins his people, still wet, but with his demeanor back. He rides high on his horse and goes through the settlement, everyone cheering him on as he passes. He raises his sword high as he takes in the appreciation he is not even sure he really deserves. But Dagda is letting him have this moment. After all, it would be absolute chaos if the people knew that they had the gods in their midst.

Ailill, Dagda, and Oenghus are in his house now, leaving everybody to do what they need to do. The people are determined to get every trace of the onslaught out of their minds as quickly as possible. The ones who have lost loved ones are already preparing for their burial; there is no need to wait. They just want to return to normal as soon as they possibly can.

A calmness now settles over the entire settlement. Everybody thanks the warriors that have come to help them, all getting different stories of where they come from, and how it is that they came to meet Cath. They are already regaling those that were not on the battlefield with tales of how they drove the Greeks and Romans into a corner, and how they slaughtered them. Their thirst for blood is obvious, so obvious that the Celts are grateful that they were on their side.

It is well past midnight, and nobody is even thinking of sleep. They are preparing for a feast in honor of their guests, and they are dancing despite the losses they have suffered today. They have decided to honor the men who lost their lives on the field of battle, and the best way to honor them is not to mourn, but to celebrate.

The sun rises the next day to find them ready for the day of feasting. The dead have been buried, and the Greeks and Romans are basically ashes on the heaps on the outskirts of the settlement. Gusts of wind have thankfully carried the smell of burning flesh away from the settlement. The Celts hope that this smell is carried to the shores of Greece, and to the cities of Rome, so that they know what happened here, and so that they know never to take such a foolish gamble again.

CHAPTER 15

BY SUNRISE, the Druids are very busy indeed. They are making sacrifices to the gods already, and the sound of their chanting echoes all across the Welsh Plain. The atmosphere is jovial, more so than just a few hours ago. The dead have been buried, and they have been mourned, although not completely. However, the magnitude of the Celtic victory has now settled completely over the entire settlement and everyone cannot help but be in a very happy mood.

The feast has begun. The Celts are providing every manner of entertainment to their visitors, anything but mock fights of course. The battle the day before certainly left a bitter taste in their mouths. The entertainment and festivities are no less spectacular, however, and the gods seem to really be enjoying themselves.

Children play in the fields again, carefree and with no more concern for their safety. Their parents are relaxed too, and they can sip leisurely on the wine and ale that fills their cups. One would almost think that this was a scene from the Otherworld, playing out in spectacular fashion in front of them. Only Cath would know this, only she would be able to make this reference. She is nowhere to be seen, however.

Cath can be found in the tent on the sidelines of the battlefield, a sponge in hand, dabbing Eogan's forehead. He has slept through the night, and she is starting to wonder if he will ever open his eyes again. The seers have assured her however that he will be okay, the herbs that they administered to Eogan having 'sleep' as a side effect, to allow him to heal quickly.

She tends to her wounded love, so many things that she wants to say to him. She just wants him to open his eyes so that she can tell him that she loves him. She just wants to hold him and feel his arms around her. Still, though, Eogan is lost in a world that is inside his head so that she is not even sure whether he knows that she is here with him.

A strange comfort comes from watching him sleeping. She is filled with happiness at the prospect of her future with him. She needs him to know this. Cath starts to tell him everything that she has experienced since she left the plains. She talks to him as though he can hear her, and soon enough she is telling him everything about her rather extraordinary adventures.

Then suddenly he opens his eyes, all be it sluggishly. He has to look at Cath for the longest time, not sure if he is just seeing what he wants to see, or if the love of his life is actually with him right now. With a little effort and a lot of pain, he reaches for her. She comes down to him so that she can settle her face in his hands, and confirm for him that she is indeed very, very real.

"Cath..." he strains to speak.

"No, don't speak, not yet. Welcome back..." She assures him that she is not going anywhere and that soon when he gets out of here, they will be married. She is suddenly very anxious about marrying Eogan, the thought of how close she came to losing him is still very present in her mind, and it is something she does not ever want to experience again.

She feeds him some fruit after giving him some water. She watches as the color returns to his face, and he starts to gain his strength back almost immediately. Then she just lies in his arms, careful to avoid his wounds, however, but still managing to get very close to her man.

Emotions start to stir in Eogan, the same emotions that have been stirring in Cath from the moment she saw Eogan on the battlefield. She isn't sleeping, with her eyes just closed as she breathes in the smell of Eogan. His eyes are open though, and he watches her closely, not sure if he will have the strength to do what he so desperately wants to do with her.

Eventually, he cannot hold himself back, and he kisses the top of her head gently. She smiles, still not opening her eyes, however. She is almost afraid that if she does, this scene will disappear, and it will all prove itself to be just a dream. When Eogan kisses her mouth, however, she knows that he is really here with her, and so she opens her eyes.

They kiss their fill of one another, locking their eyes on each other. Their intensity magnifies with each moment that passes, and soon Eogan's pain fades into the background so that it is a dull lull somewhere in the back of his mind. He makes slow and deliberate work of Cath's dress, and then he props himself upon his arm, enjoying the view, and enjoying her feel, running his fingers down her body, and then up again.

He kisses her all over while removing the clothing that covers the parts of him that he will need for the completion of his conquest. Cath helps him until they are both completely naked. A steady breeze blows through the tent, cooling them, but not blowing so hard as to threaten their privacy.

Eogan continues to kiss Cath, touching every part of her body with his lips. He moves over her with a sensuality that he himself wasn't sure he could muster given his condition. The human mind is proving to be a remarkable organ, however, and the matter at hand seems to have won hands down over what he knows his situation is in his mind.

They lock in the places on their bodies that have craved each other for the longest time now. The connection is hot, and they start to fulfill each other in ways that they have never experienced before. They are locked in passionate lovemaking now, answering with their bodies every single question that the pair has had for each other.

Back at the settlement, everyone is still enjoying the festivities. They are also quite drunk now, and the gods find the humans amusing. They also know that they have to leave soon, their work here is done. The Druids and the seers have offered them sufficient thanks and praise so that they are satisfied. Ailill however, still feels that he needs to appease the gods in some way for letting him keep Cath.

"There is no need for you to do anything more than you have already done, but thank you anyway for making the offer!" Dagda really wants to get back to the Otherworld now, so that he can focus on getting his son back into the game of life. He just needs to be reminded of everything that he has so that he can quickly forget what he has lost.

"Thank you..." Ailill manages, and the two men shake on it. Cath's father makes a deal with the gods, that they will enjoy the protection of the gods, as long as they continue to observe every festival, every ritual to the gods. This seems fair enough, and after a moment, the gods start to gather themselves and get ready to leave this place.

Oenghus looks around for Cath, but he still doesn't see her. He has not seen her all day actually, and he knows where she is. He wonders what they must be doing, secluded and alone in the tent, but he very quickly shakes this thought from his head. He does not want to think of Cath in that position with another man. He too is suddenly anxious to get back to the life that he knows, and to the distraction of the nymphs he knows will be very happy to have him back alone, and all to themselves.

Cath doesn't think of Oenghus however, how can she. There are a million thoughts going on in her head, and each one of them has to do with the man who is moving gently on top of her, and inside her. She cannot contain herself, as tears of joy start streaming down her face. She is just so incredibly happy.

Eogan too has many emotions. All of them center around the woman underneath him, with so much love flowing from every part of her body. They are truly one now, together, and moving seamlessly through time and space, so that the moment seems to be suspended. Not a second passes, and they just keep on enjoying each other, more and more, moment to beautiful moment. It is really incredible.

The gods look over the Welsh Plains for the last time, before they start to march out. They need to get away from the settlement before Dagda opens up the porthole to the Otherworld, out of view of the human beings. They just don't need the added complication of the humans knowing that they are actually among them and that they have been since the battle, fighting with them on the field.

They bid farewell to the Celts, and start their diligent march into the distance. They just have to get over the horizon, and then they will be free to open up the gateway to their home. The gods are excited to be going home, as are their warriors. However, they cannot hide the fact that they had a very good time amongst the Celts, especially during the battle.

The Celts cheer and wave as they start to move out. Some of the Celts even follow them, at least part of the way, just to see them off well. Although, from their performance the day before, there is now worry about their capabilities to protect themselves. Some of the Celts are starting to feel that at least some of them should stay behind to help them, although there is no chance of the Greeks and Romans coming back any time soon.

The Celts accompanying the gods wave them farewell and then make their way back to the settlement. All the Celts continue with the celebrations well into the night, and then they all go to their individual homes to reconnect with their families. Smoke comes up from the chimneys again, and a level of contentment is felt through every corner of the land.

The men in the settlement kiss their children goodnight and embrace them. They hold their wives and the women they love, and they also confirm this love using their bodies. The atmosphere in the settlement is soaked in lovemaking now, and none of them, not a single couple, can even come close to Cath and Eogan, who are still loving each other physically, and emotionally.

Ailill has nobody to love tonight, however, and he does not even care. He just appreciates the success that they have enjoyed, and he is just happy that life on the plains can go back to normal. He takes his contentment with him to bed, and he actually falls asleep very quickly so that he is sure that he will get a very good night's rest. There is no stress of strain in him at all anymore, and this is a beautiful feeling, one that he has not felt for a very long time.

Eogan and Cath just look at each other now, lying side by side, Cath's head on Eogan's chest. There is no need for words, and so they are both just quiet, with the biggest smiles on their faces. Thoughts are aplenty in their minds, however, but it is okay for them not to say what they are thinking. There is just no need for them to break this beautiful moment with words.

Cath is still tingling from the fingers that are running up and down her body so that soon she is ready for Eogan to take her again. He is also ready, wanting her more than he just did, and feeling like he could ravage her forever. They do not hold themselves back at all, taking each other again, and enjoying it every bit as they just did.

When they eventually emerge from the tent, it is almost sunset on the second day. Cath is amazed by what she sees. Everything seems to have returned to normal quite quickly. The ashes of the burned-out bodies have been carried off by the wind. She can almost see new grass growing in the places where Celts fell during the battle. There is the sense that new life is coming up out of the earth, to coincide with the new life that the Celts will now enjoy.

Eogan too is impressed with what he sees. He cannot believe his eyes. Even his injuries seem to have healed rather quickly, and the places where he was cut are just a mild itch now. At least there is no infection so that he knows that he is going to make a full recovery. They both make their way back to the settlement, and they find Ailill's house, where he is standing in the front of the house, a large crowd gathering outside.

Cath goes up to her father and embraces him. Everybody watches them with their arms around each other, and they admire this affection. They bow their heads to Cath, in appreciation for what she has done for them. Cath takes in their appreciation quietly, with no need to say anything. She stands with Eogan and Ailill to her left and right, and they all look over the crowd that is looking at all of them, half expecting a speech, and half not.

Ailill takes this opportunity to thank everyone, for their commitment, and for their sacrifice. He also lets them know that everything going forward is going be peace in the land and that the people don't have to worry about any more wars. He says this confidently, remembering the last conversation that he had with Dagda. Assurances were exchanged between them, and he knows that when Eogan takes over the leadership of these people, he will continue to observe every ritual and continue to offer up praise to the gods.

He takes his family inside the house now, knowing that Eogan needs to rest, and knowing that he also needs to be close to Cath. He admires the choices that she has made in her life, and the time when she did not listen to him, even though at the time he really wished she had. He watches them interact with one another, and he knows that there is love here. Ailill is confident that Eogan is the best man to take care of his daughter, and that his daughter will make a good and loyal wife to this nobleman.

The crowd has dispersed outside the house now. They can go on with their lives, with the assurance that everything will be okay now. Yes, they suffered great losses, but the sacrifices that they made have been worth it. Everyone thinks of the strength it must have taken for Cath to come back to the war, and they admire her even more than they did before, not thinking that this was even possible. It is, however, and the people are glad to have a princess of the caliber that Cath has shown. She is truly a gem.

As she prepares dinner for the two men in her life, she thinks of how everything played out. She remembers all the choices she had to make before she had to leave her home. She remembers the choices that she made when she was trekking through the wilderness on her way to Scotland. Cath remembers all the choices she had to make in the Otherworld, and she regrets the promise that she did not keep, for her own reasons.

How could she keep this promise, though, when her life is here? This is the only life she knows. It is the only life she wants. She cannot imagine life without Eogan, or her father. She knows that Oenghus will be okay. She just has to believe it. There is really no other way for this to have turned out. She cannot think what the gods must be saying about her. However, she cannot be too bothered by this right now.

As she serves dinner to Ailill and Eogan she confirms for herself that she made the correct choices. Every decision led her to the next one, and they all fused together to create this beautiful outcome that she now gets to enjoy. She makes the conscious choice not to regret anything that she has done, or to be remorseful of anything that she has not done. Choices are what make us human, after all, and Cath is happy with hers.

She wonders about her horse though...

ABOUT THE AUTHOR

Johana Gardener is an emerging erotica author of many erotica kinks and sub-genres. Be sure to check out other books and leave a review if this story got you hot!

Visit my blog at Johana Gardener Blog

Join my newsletter for exclusive Johana Gardener Newsletter

Sign up for Free Stories from Xplicit Press Authors

Xplicit Press Author Updates

Like Xplicit Press on Facebook

Follow Xplicit Press on Twitter

Readers: I want to expand a few of the stories to see where the characters can be explored further. If there are any of the stories that you would like to read more about again, I'd love to hear from you!

Keep In Touch
Johana Gardener
info@johanagardener.com